"A free-wheeling, fast-paced hippie fantasy
of one young man's search
for meaning in life."
– *Kirkus Reviews*

Acid Head Buddha

Also available in Japanese

Written & Translated by Anthony Lojac

Think More Books

Beverly Hills

Publisher's Cataloging-In-Publication Data
(Prepared by The Donohue Group, Inc.)

Lojac, Anthony.
  Acid Head Buddha / by Anthony Lojac.

      pages : cm.

Issued also as an ebook.
ISBN-13: 978-0-9818604-3-5
ISBN-10: 0-9818604-3-5
Library of Congress Control Number: 2015900947
Think More Books, Beverly Hills, California

  1. Hippies--Travel--Fiction. 2. Man-woman relationships--Fiction. 3. Cults--California--Los Angeles--Fiction. 4. Wisdom--Fiction. 5. Reincarnation--Fiction. 6. Humorous stories. 7. Erotic stories. I. Title.

PS3562.O512 A35 2015
813/.54
                    ThinkMoreBooks *Beverly Hills*
                     www.thinkmorebooks.com

Acid Head Buddha

Think More Books

Beverly Hills

Acid Head Buddha

Anthony Lojac

Contents

~Part Three~
In The City of Angels

~Part Four~
In The Other City of Angels

~Part Five~
In The Eastern Capital

~Part Six~
In The Here & Now

Acid Head Buddha is the story
of a young man's experience
in this life and the afterlife
on a quest for eternal love.

Part One: In The Beginning

1. The Word

2. The Mirror

~1~

The Word

In the beginning, we are told by the wisest of our tribe, was The Word.

No space. No blackness. Nothing.

From Nothing, comes Something.

A beat, a pulse in empty darkness.

Buh dum, buh dum, buh dum.

Buh dum, buh dum, buh dum.

Then, as now, The Word *A~U~M* reverberates through all space for those who have ears to hear, forever, until the end of time.

There, in that limitless virgin space, a single dot of light appears and explodes into violent action.

Whether it took not one single instant of time, or it took ten billion trillion years, means nothing at all.

It just is the way it is, in our universe.

Everything comes from The First Star.

All imaginable geometry of being, and the entirety of historical existence, all come from The First Star.

~2~

The Mirror

Now, on December 6, 1969, one speck of light shines like a star on the tip of incense burning on a makeshift mystic altar. Trippy sitar music is playing on the turntable. There is a young man's face, mouth agape, with big brown eyes dilated in the candlelit room.

Speakers support homemade bookshelves with the young man's altar and mirror.

His face is in that mirror on that altar, staring, searching for itself through rippling incense smoke.

He has long brown hair, an athletic build. He is almost a typical 18-year old hippie in a typical hippie room, but something is special.

The energy is visible, palpable.

He is connected to the universe.

Subtle chakra energy sparkles for one instant into the shape of a caduceus, two entwined serpents facing each other, with angel type wings radiating around his shoulders.

***

GENETIC FREEMAN says:

"I am that young man.

I see myself sitting there…

I understand here and now…

Everything is vibrating.

Everything is alive."

Part Two:
In The Western Capital

3. The Beat Goes On

4. Slick & Beautiful

5. Acid Love

6. Hold On Tight

~3~

The Beat Goes On

Outside, the usual hip and colorful Greenwich Village scene is happening around Washington Square.

The Hare Krishna group is singing and dancing.

The old beatnik bum, ONE EYE JOHNNY, needs a crutch to stand up, but continues to be amused by it all as he conducts an animated argument with a couple Black Panthers.

ALLISON, the hot young girl with peach colored hair, is in a neat blue skirt and sheer white blouse, standing in front of a folding table with books on it.

She tries to hand out red papers to everyone walking by, asking anyone who will listen, "Do you want to find out who you really are?"

SLICK WILLIE, slender young Black guy dressed like an inexplicably euphoric whore, just smiles at her as he prances by and declines one of her handouts.

Two guys in blue slacks and white shirts stand sharp behind that table, by a poster for PSYTRON, watching everything Allison does.

***

I'm getting ready to go out.

I grab some books and tuck them into my purple bag:

"The Tibetan Book of the Dead,"

"Doors of Perception," and

"The Psychedelic Experience."

I leave "Woodstock Nation" and "Naked Lunch" out on the table.

I tie up my hand-painted day-glow red, high-top Converse, matching my yellow and red T-shirt from Village Bookstore.

I pick up Naked Lunch.

I talk to myself in the mirror.

"In the beginning, was The Word..."

I look at the book.

"But you say language is a virus from outer space."

I look up, through the smoke, deeper into my own eyes again…

✶✶✶

I cannot explain what I see.

I can only say it.

In Mexico City, on September 6, 1951, three months before we were born, a happily intoxicated lady sips a martini she is holding in one hand, and places an apple on top of her head with her other hand.

William Burroughs lowers his arm at the target.

He aims.

He fires.

He shoots his cool young wife, JOAN, in the head.

The martini glass falls first, and shatters on the floor.

Joan hits the floor next, still smiling, even with a bullet hole in the middle of her head.

The apple rolls to the fore.

✶✶✶

When Joan's ethereal body becomes visible, she is confused and near panic. She hears a woman's voice. It is special, a God-like voice.

"Calm down dear. Everything is going to be alright."

It is grey and hazy inside the industrial-size, between-lives processing facility, run by the LIZARD LADY.

Joan asks, "What happened?"

The Lizard Lady tells her, "Bill shot you in the head."

Joan thinks, "He said something." she tries to remember what he said. "But I can't remember his words, or even his language."

Joan keeps looking around, trying to figure out where she is.

Sparks and wisps of electricity are flying around the Lizard Lady, an aristocratic woman with a buxom Marylyn-type upper body.

The Lizard Lady says, "Yes, I understand."

Joan realizes what is happening.

"Please, don't make me a girl again."

The Lizard Lady pats Joan sympathetically with her bejeweled fingers, and manicured nails.

"Life does have to go on, even after you're dead, of course."

The Lizard Lady smiles.

"You know what I mean Joan."

The Lizard Lady has a suspiciously reptilian lower body in the dark.

Joan begs, "Please... No..."

The Lizard Lady tells her, "You need to get ready again dear. The second half of the 20th century is going to be a real lollapalooza!"

~4~

Slick & Beautiful

I step outside, almost-cool-as-I-think-I-am, singing Dylanesque as I bop through the neighborhood in my red sneakers and brown motorcycle jacket.

"Take me on a trip upon your magic swirlin' ship..."

Yeah, I'm feeling good.

I nod to friends on my way to Washington Square.

"I'm ready to go anywhere..."

An Ominous Minister from The Church of The Final End, in black hooded robe and blood-red lining, is on the hunt for new meat.

He asks me, "Are you ready for The End?"

I give him the peace sign, and keep singing, "I'm ready for to fade…"

The Ominous Minister continues spitting out his words at me, "This is The End my friend. The End!"

I keep walking, looking for my man.

I hear the Minister yelling after me, "Ride the highway west baby, ride the snake!"

I ignore the Jim Morrison wannabe, and keep looking for my man. He got something special for me today.

There he is, Slick Willie.

Tall and thin. Walks like an Egyptian.

Slick Willie sees me too, "Free Man! Wha's happening."

We maneuver through people-traffic, to each other.

"Hey! Wha's happening Slick."

"Gonna be colder than the…"

"It's not even cold Willie, you just like to say nipple on a witch's tit."

Willie dances around, laughing the way he does, then sticks his middle finger up into my face, close to my mouth, "Happy Birthday."

When we were kids, Slick Willie was the first openly homosexual guy I knew.

One day between classes, he asks me to jerk off in a cup, bring it to school. Says he'll drink it.

I almost gag. I think he can't be serious. He must be trying to gross me out on purpose.

He says, "Suck it off man!"

Walk li-i-ike an E-gyp-tian.

I see a tiny piece of colored paper on his fingertip.

"It's pure right?"

Willie sings like Sly Stone. "Gonna take you higher."

"No speed or anything?"

He looks me in the eyes. "You ain't never gonna come down."

"Humm."

"Suck it off man! 'fore I fuckin' absorb it into my skin or something!"

I carefully peel the paper off Willie's fingertip.

Walk li-i-ike an E-gyp-tian.

I suck my own finger off real good.

Willie laughs and sings, "Yeah baby, don'tcha, don'tcha, don'tcha wanna get higher."

I tell him, "Boom laka-laka-laka Willie, I gotta get to Village Books before this stuff kicks in."

He looks at the purple sack on my shoulder. "Free Man, you the only guy I know take books to da book store."

"You trippin' Willie? I'm the only guy you know goes to a book store."

We laugh.

The Hare Krishna group comes by dancing and singing, "Hare Krishna, Hare Krishna, Krishna Krishna, Hare Hare, Hare Rama, Hare Rama, Rama Rama, Hare Hare..."

One guy shows me an illustration of reincarnation from lower animals to higher humans, "Do you believe in reincarnation?"

I tell him, "I don't have to believe in reincarnation my brother. I *remember* it."

One of the Krishna girls smiles at me and says, "Hare Krishna."

I smile too, and give her the peace sign.

I turn back to Willie, "This stuff is pure right?"

✶✶✶

Something catches my eye.

That hot young girl, she's watching me again.

She sees I'm not going to walk by her table.

She comes after me as I'm walking away.

Allison reaches out to give me one of those red papers from Psytron, "Do you want to find out who you really are?"

Naturally, I stare at her nipples.

She knows, as well as I, she is too hot for me to ignore.

I ask, "For me?"

She says, "Just for you."

I take the paper, feel her magical hair slide across my fingers, and I look up into her eyes, "Ah, thanks…"

A passerby bumps between us. People quickly fill the space, walking in front of me, interrupting the conversation. Allison scurries to protect her position, and speaks like we are old friends already. "Wanna go to a lecture?"

I see a subtle flash of energy out of dime-size black holes in two balls of electromagnetic white gel.

"Ah…"

"I'm Allison."

"Cool."

"Do you know who you are?"

"Yeah, I mean, sure."

Allison waits for elaboration.

I look happily dumb.

"Wanna be who you really are forever, and ever, and ever?"

"Say what?"

Her energy sparkles.

I search her eyes deeper.

She tells me, "I like your eyes Genetic. They are so big!"

"You too, your eyes are like amazing!"

Allison's eyeball energy arches right into my pupils. She takes my arm, and we walk away together.

That's right, I think to myself, I'm Genetic Freeman! Lotta people know my name around here.

✳✳✳

We approach a building. I see signs in the window: *Psytron* and *Find Out Who You Really Are* and *Be Who You Really Are, Forever!*

I have to tell her, "Like, I don't have any money."

She smiles. Walks me inside, holding my hand, and leads me into a room with rows of chairs on an incline to a podium.

The Speaker is an energetic little guy drawing diagrams on a white-board under a big poster of some guy by a jet.

I am in the middle of the front row, too nervous to look and see if anyone else is actually there to hear this.

The Speaker points up at the poster and announces, "Ladies and Gentlemen, this is: Regulator One!"

The little guy just beams with pride, "Regulator One is going to change your life!"

All I see is a big picture of a middle age white guy who is also very proud of himself and his jet too.

"Regulator One developed Psytron Theological Technology to help you find out who you really are, and help you be who you really are, forever!"

The Speaker stops, and waits for amazement from his audience.

I peek around, still can't see anyone else, so I throw the guy a bone, "Far out man."

The Speaker is satisfied. He proceeds to draw more details on the white-board.

I continue to act like I might possibly care, and I try not to freak out.

~5~

Acid Love

Back in my room. The candles are lit. Sitar and percussion are playing on the turntable, *West Meets East*, Ravi Shankar with Yehudi Menuhin on violin.

I sit.

I pour tea into unmatched cups as best I can.

I stare at my own cup too long.

Allison observes patiently.

"It's macrobiotic," I finally say.

Allison sips, smiles approvingly.

I add, "From Japan."

"So, how did you like the lecture Genetic?"

"Umm, maybe the little guy talks about the big guy too much but..."

Allison frowns.

I perspire.

"Ah, but it was really good I mean."

She says, "Psytron Theological Technology is based on manipulation of the electromagnetic structure of the human aura."

"That's what he said! Ah, I think."

"Didn't he tell you about the Holy Conman too?"

"Yeah, that Holy Man thing..."

"Holy Conman!" She corrects me, and elucidates.

"Some people say it is God. But I think it is *Ha Satan*, the Devil."

I tell Allison, "I'm trying to dig it... You mean, like Sympathy for the Devil or something? Like Mick, or, or, even Keith, is really the…"

She says, "Genetic, are you like flipping out?"

I struggle how to answer, and then blurt out.

"I'm eighteen. Yeah, today is my birthday."

Allison chokes on her own surprise before she can speak, "There's something happening here."

I look left and right and back at her, "What?"

She says, "Today is my birthday too."

Now that really blows my mind.

Sparks go off between our auras, dancing back and forth, connecting and intertwining our energies more deeply.

I tell her, "We gotta get outta this place."

I am slow, but I get ready to almost get up to go.

Allison looks at me more closely, and says, "We?"

I blush. "Ah, yeah…" And then, I have a brainstorm. "Come to Frisco with me! Hippie Heaven! On my bike!"

Allison blushes now too, and notices the mattress.

She is most helpful at clarification of my intent, "You mean you don't want to go to bed first?"

"Oh... Yeah. I forgot! Let's spend the night together…"

"…Now?" she asks, shuffling over, laughing, as I sit back down from almost getting up.

We start making out.

The electromagnetic energy is visible, firing through our chakras as we make love, intense, peak-out, ecstatic love, on the cushions and table in front of my mirror.

We pay no mind to books and things falling off the shelves.

✳✳✳

Early next morning, I'm still asleep with Allison on my single mattress.

I see myself in a lucid dream, with a girl suspended in space outside my window. I fly out to inspect her, and run my fingers through her shining hair.

She is surreal. Her electromagnetic vibrations are pulsing too fast.

Or are those my vibrations?

I tell myself, "It's just a dream. I'm going to relax and wake up slow."

But when I open my eyes, the girl is sitting in a dark room I do not know.

She says, "All that we see or seem, is but a dream within a dream."

"I'm sorry, but... What?"

She says, "Beautiful words aren't they. But Edgar Allan Poe was wrong."

Candles alight all over the room.

The girl morphs into a WICKED OLD WITCH on a Magic Throne, in a Gypsy Room.

I see magical and mysterious symbols on her and all around her. She has obvious mastery of all occult techniques and paraphernalia.

Then, the Wicked Old Witch really blows my mind and says, "I'm so happy to see you again."

***

I am shocked awake with eyes wide open.

I read the headlines firing into my eyeballs:

Violence at Altamont is The End of Hippie Heaven!

"Angels kill people at a free concert while Mick is singing Sympathy for the Devil?"

"I knew it! I fucking knew it!"

Could this really be The End?

~6~

Hold On Tight

The Sun is hiding today. People are on the hustle in NYC, taking care of their business before it rains.

I'm in sunglasses for the ride, and a bandana tied like a belt around my head. Securing my purple bag and gear on my bike.

Allison is styling in designer jeans, new leather jacket, and her bandana over her hair.

Slick Willie says, "You gonna be cool in LA man?"

One Eye Johnny watches, laughing.

I say, "Oh yeah, I'm gonna be real cool."

Willie shakes his head in half-pretend disapproval.

Allison says, "We're in love Willie! We want to be together forever!"

Willie tells her, "They crazy in Frisco. They more crazy in LA."

One Eye Johnny says, "Dig the scene in MacArthur Park man, that's where the coolest of the cool cats congregate."

I say, "MacArthur Park, yeah, I'll dig it."

He says, "And take that fucking cake man! Bake it, fake it, do whatever you got to do, but take that fucking cake out the rain!"

Allison looks like she wants to say something to Johnny, but nothing seems to make enough sense.

I'm not sure about the cake, but I am certainly determined to be as cool as I can be in LA.

I nod to Johnny, give him a touch on the shoulder.

Then, it's time to go.

I straddle my bike.

Things automatically feel more exciting with my bike between my legs.

I give it a good kick-start, and zip up my leather jacket.

Allison climbs on behind me, grabs on to her man nice and tight.

I look at my good friend Willie, give the peace sign, shift into gear, and ride off with my books and my beautiful old lady.

Part Three:
In The City of Angels

7. Regulator One

8. When You're Stranger

9. Wai Yu

~7~

Regulator One

I come blasting out of the tunnel, riding through Griffith Park, with Allison holding on behind me.

We are worn out of course, but happy we survived the ride cross-country.

We stop. Try looking through the smog.

It's exactly like they say it is, dirty and yellow.

We can't see much at all.

But we do see the Hollywood Sign, and the sprawling complexes of Psytron facilities.

***

Time passes quickly out here.

Allison gets pretty deep into Psytron during our first couple years in LA. Works her way up the organization. Does all kind of secret, high-level stuff.

I don't like it much, but I can't do anything about it either.

***

The intense guy from the poster with the jet, sits behind his desk, lights a smoke, and scrutinizes his lovely young acolyte.

ELIZABETH, his wife and Chief of Security, sits on top of the desk, talks with clicking tension in her jaw.

"Jesus wanted to use His divine power to give Mary Magdalene a male soul, to fix her, make her a man."

Allison feels nauseous, but says what she was trained to say. "I ate the same apple again, and again, and again."

They are all in their blue Psytron uniforms.

Allison looks good in her skirt and sheer blouse with her hot nipples, but she is not quite the same glowing young seductress she used to be in NYC.

Elizabeth continues, "When Eve ate the apple and gave it to Adam…"

Regulator One shoves his face forward. "The eyes of both of them were opened, and they discovered they were naked."

Allison answers crisply, "Yes Sir, I do understand."

Elizabeth explains, "God said, Behold, the man has become as one of us, to know Good and Evil."

Regulator One takes over again, asking Allison, "God is plural, do you see? He says us, us!"

"I understand. God is plural, more than one."

Regulator One leans his head back and exhales thick smoke before he speaks again.

"The sequence is equally important."

Allison says, "Yes Sir. The woman has already given her man Knowledge of Good and Evil. But God continues…"

Elizabeth finishes for her, "Now, lest he put forth his hand and take also of the Tree of Life and eat and live forever, let us send him forth from the Garden of Eden."

Allison says, "We've had knowledge of Good and Evil for a long time, but we haven't had Eternal Life until now."

Regulator One almost smiles, "Bingo!"

Elizabeth says, "God prevented woman from enticing man into Eternal Life!"

Regulator One reminds Allison, "God doesn't like what we do here."

Allison knows what she has to say.

"What can I do, now, I mean, about God?"

~8~

When You're Stranger

I walk into a bizarre version of the Last Supper, with all kind of mystic guru freaks on stage at the head table.

Twin Indian Snake Charmers sit back-to-back, legs crossed, playing identical music to charm their respective Cobras out of their respective baskets.

A stone statue transmutates into a live demon, a woman's face on a serpentine body.

Legs fall from a table, hissing as they slither away.

I have Family at one table and Friends at another, but I rush over to a table full of Strangers, to which I am beckoned.

I am confronted with models and other beautiful people, hungry for someone significantly less beautiful than they are, someone they can enjoy showing themselves to.

The Beautiful Woman tells me, "We know exactly what you think of yourself."

The Beautiful Man explains, "Such measurements are the precious currency of our chosen trade."

A *Newbie* Beautiful Young Man trying to squeeze his chair into the circle around the table says, "Isn't it so terribly dreadful how ordinary people can interfere with one's enjoyment of one's own beauty."

All the Beautiful People go 'Ohh' and 'Ahh' and move their chairs to accommodate the sweet young thing at their table.

"What a lovely sentiment!" says one Matronly Beauty.

"Are you a Philosopher?" asks a Beautiful Young Lady.

Naked babies are lying on the cold floor. Petrified.

"I think I am," says the Beautiful Newbie.

The difference between self and others is too clear.

I move along, past other tables, the nervous Liars and Frauds, and the Killers.

And then, there he is, MR. JONES.

A bookish white guy is sitting all alone in the corner. Pointing his crooked finger at me. Speaking words and gibberish, "You! You Mr. Free Man! You did this to everyone, it is all your fault!"

I approach cautiously, sit down with Mr. Jones and say, "I can sit here and think about the difference between what I see and all that I have been shown."

"You Genetic, you, it is your fault! All your fault!"

"Don't blame me!"

Mr. Jones thinks again.

"You mean, you ain't the one in charge?"

"I just look at what I see."

The wave-particle duality of light.

The wave-particle duality of matter.

The universal primary phenomenon is not a wave and is not a particle.

He says, "Your vision gets in the way of your vision."

I say, "My brain has a hundred billion neurons, each as complete as the most sophisticated computer, each connected to ten thousand other neurons."

He says, "Norepinephrine is a prehistoric chemical found in the nerve-like cells of the crab, spider, and worm. It is also found in the otherwise empty spaces of our own embryonic skulls. It attracts cells from our earliest lizard-like brain formation, causing them to float up and organize into complex hierarchies, settle down, and produce axons to weave into the fabric of our higher cortex."

I say, "I should know these things."

He says, "Think about the electromagnetic formation of the processes and objects of reality."

I think I understand, beneath the molecular level, biology disappears and there is only physics.

I say again, "I should know these things."

But I don't really know what it all means.

I think I absorb too much from people around me. I'm not sure where my edges are.

★★★

And then, time slips again before I realize it.

Now I got some drunk freckle-face REDNECK slobbering all over me.

"Fuckin' Niggers shot my brother through the head in jail."

Red pulls me tight, kisses my cheek.

I pull away.

He keeps talking, "I know who my enemies are."

I tell him, "Yeah, yeah, real good for you."

He says, "I beat a faggot in the men's room too. Stuck his head in the toilet. Held him down, made him choke for air."

"What did you say before you stuck his face in the toilet? You test him, the way you test me?"

"Faggot gave me the wrong answer."

"Yeah, sure… I let people think whatever they want, ya know. I don't care you think I'm a faggot or not."

Red says, "Fuckin' faggot."

"I know you think I'm stupid because I don't hate Black people too."

He goes off on Elvis again, the way he does, all of a sudden. "The King, I love the King man."

"Again? Oh come on…"

"You say something 'bout the king I'll fuck you up."

Red puffs up into attack mode.

"Listen, I just don't care. That's all. I heard all about your Elvis story already."

Red deflates, with tears in his eyes.

"He died man, it's so sad."

"I'm worried about myself. I can't live in this world anymore with people like you."

Red wipes his eyes, "You're too fuckin' weak."

I tell him straight, "There's too much hate inside you. People like you are too violent."

He tells me straight too, "You're just a pussy."

***

Freckle-face Redneck attacks as soon as his target walks out of a long dark tunnel in MacArthur Park, back into the rain, with a wet cake in his left hand.

Red picked the wrong guy tonight.

VINNEY COLD KILLER is a 30ish white guy, in a grey suit, with a face hard as his name. He confronts the attacker correctly, with no weakness showing and not one instant of hesitation.

The cake plops down to the ground.

There is a subtle movement of his right wrist: tight muscular threads lift the palm backward, turn the tubular wooden handle one-quarter around, place the needle-sharp point on the attacker's left eyelid, produce a slight indentation in skin, then a barely perceptible flick, up and down, and a liquid red X appears in the middle of Red's eyelid.

The needle-sharp point comes down again, to rest on the X. And VCK tells this unfortunate villain, "If you can't figure out instantly, despite your expectations, it is not you, but I who am in control, you will die."

Red is scared half to death.

And for the other half…

Lightning strikes, his bowels explode, his head jerks forward, and his left eye is skewered on the pick.

~9~

Wai Yu

I ride out of the mountains in Griffith Park, back into the smog, down Alvarado and past MacArthur Park.

I cut the engine in front of an old Victorian home, throw my jacket over my shoulder and nod to a new friend who is watching my every move.

WAI YU waves back like a little girl from the big front porch.

He sees my windblown hair, tight jeans, yellow and red T-shirt from Bodhi Tree Books, and my new leather belt with cool Indian-head nickels on it.

I look at this frail and pale monk, wrapped in saffron, and I want to yell at everyone in the world, "Why don't we all be like him?"

***

I follow Wai Yu inside.

The dark wood is painted red, pink, orange, yellow and purple. Colors the Good Ghosts and Hippies prefer.

I leave my riding boots inside by the door, follow Wai Yu down the hall into his room, sit on a cushion, sip tea when it is offered, and feel Wai Yu caress me with his eyes like a mystic lover.

He speaks softly, "Tell me more about who you think you really are."

"It is not so easy for me, Wai Yu."

He says, "If it were easy, I believe it would be too difficult for you."

I ponder that, and I think, if I understand correctly, he may be right.

Then, I feel my attention being pulled over to Psytron Headquarters.

***

Regulator One is talking to Elizabeth, "Is this acid head character going to be a problem?"

She says, "He's too stupid to be a problem."

Regulator One glares.

"But of course, Allison loved him. So maybe she talked."

He continues his glare.

"It is very easy to die on a motorcycle in LA."

His glare lessens noticeably.

✶✶✶

I tell Wai Yu, "Bad people want to kill me here in the City of Angels."

That possibility terrifies the gentle monk.

I say, "And I'm in love with a ghost."

Then, Wai Yu has me stand.

He prostrates himself at my feet, face down on top of my socks.

The gentle monk kisses my feet.

I wish my feet were clean.

He kisses my feet again.

I exhale, and I really wish my feet were clean.

Wai Yu says, "You don't know who you are?"

"I... I... I..."

He doesn't wait for my answer.

He knows I don't know.

He kisses my feet, bends his neck way back, looks up and says, "This is what it is like to be me."

I exhale air I forgot I had.

Wai Yu allows me to sit again and listen to his story.

"I escape from Vietnam, run away to Thailand, work for Old Monk."

Wai Yu seems lost in thought for a few seconds.

I try to help, "Ah, like some special monk work?"

Wai Yu tries to focus, and with visible effort says, "He will make The Perfect Buddha's Head. Yes, from a sacred piece of Yew."

Now this is a bitch. I hate to interrupt again but, "Um, I'm sorry, you said a piece of me?"

Then Wai Yu is puzzled, so he speaks more clearly, "Need Sacred Yew for Perfect Head."

I decide to avoid further linguistic difficulty. So I say, "Ah, okay, I can dig it. I think, yeah."

Wai Yu is satisfied. He thinks if I can dig it he can dig it. And I think if he can dig it, then I can dig it too.

He says, "He will be immortal, live forever."

I tell him right away, "I can dig that too!"

Wai Yu says, "Although I am deeply perplexed at my own existence, I am not afraid to live my own life."

I kind of mumble to myself, "Different strokes for different folks."

He says, "Pardon?"

I say, "Got to do your own thing Wai Yu."

I smile and pour tea, refilling both our cups.

He says, "My own sense of destiny is nothing but an illusion. My own Karma is nothing but insubstantial Maya phenomena."

I say, "You got yourself together man. You're an Enlightened Master, I mean, you came here to help us in the City of Angels, right?"

"Well, I believe you did get all kind of fucked up here..."

I cannot disagree with my friend's comment.

I wait.

He says, "However, if I were you..."

I'm waiting, "Yeah...?"

He says, "Perhaps I should say, you are in the wrong City of Angels?"

"Oh, really?" I ask him, "There is another?"

Part Four:
In The Other City of Angels

~10~

Insane Husband

On December 5, 1980, in a modest Honolulu residence, a sneaky young white guy is leaving his Japanese-American wife crying at home.

"Please don't go, don't leave me alone today."

But he insists. "As the biblically authorized male head of this household, I can take care of everyone! Me, you, and *the little people* too."

Suspicious firefly wisps of energy dance around his body.

"Please don't go!"

He says, "You see *the little people* now?"

"I believe you dear! I believe the Bible can take care of everything too."

Flickering wisps of energy pass through and around him.

"I need to use my Bible now."

"Yes dear, yes, please use your Bible."

He carries his Bible into the bedroom, and closes the door.

He takes off his clothes and sits down on the floor naked, exposing himself to unseen eyes and unknown entities from another world.

The little people are all excited.

He desecrates all that his wife thinks he holds sacred, draining himself over the Bible in a series of ecstatic spasms, giving himself to the demons, praying for the evil power to kill what he cannot understand.

Then, he closes the Bible.

The little people are satisfied.

And the Husband is exactly as insane as he was before he jerked off.

★★★

I sit next to the sneaky Husband at the Honolulu airport.

I nod hello, and shift my purple bag to the other shoulder so it doesn't get in his way.

He says, "Demons are fighting for your soul."

"Say what?"

He repeats, "Demons are fighting for your soul."

"Yo dude, I'm cool."

And what the fuck, I brag a little. "I sold my bike in LA. I'm flying to Krung Thep, the mysterious City of Angels, Bangkok, Thailand!"

The guy is not impressed. "The demons will fight for your soul there too."

"Yeah, anyway, I gotta get outta this place, ya know?"

The Husband motions for me to come close.

"You escaping just in time brah. Things only getting worse here."

I tell him, "Yeah, I wanna be flying over the International Date Line on my birthday, ya know, be kind of cool."

He says, "That's just an imaginary line, ya know?"

I give him an understanding shrug on that, but can't resist saying back, "A lot of things are just imaginary."

He comes even closer. I feel his breath on my face. He says, "Let me ask ya wise guy, what one equals one?"

I think. I try to clarify, "You mean, like nothing from nothing leaves nothing?"

The Husband pulls away. "You think life means nothing?"

"No man, I mean the way you say it, it sounds like one and one and one is three or something, ya know, like John Lennon..."

He gets riled up. "I ain't John Lennon brah! I say it the way it is, that's the way I say it."

Okay, I think harder, faster, look straight back and say, "One equals one."

The guy is duly impressed.

He pulls me close again, "Listen up Cracker Jack, there's a lot more to life than one equals one."

I am equally duly impressed with this wisdom.

"Far Fucking Out."

He tells me, "It is not my problem that the rest of the world isn't ready to deal with my unique and powerful Karma."

I say, "Yeah, I can dig that too."

Then he gets on his plane and flies east to NYC, my hometown, and the nerve center of the Western World.

✶✶✶

He aims at an easy target.

He shoots him in the back with five hollow-point bullets exploding out of a Charter Arms .38 revolver on December 8, 1980.

The doorman at the Dakota knocks away his gun.

He sits on the sidewalk and waits for the police.

The little people sparkle and dance with glee.

The Doorman yells at him, "Do you know what you've just done?"

Mark David Chapman says, "Yes, I just shot John Lennon."

And somewhere on the other side of the International Date Line, I say, "I knew it! I fucking knew it!"

~11~

What Happened?

Allison's Mother is at her door, yelling in my face. "What happened to my daughter?"

"I don't know what…"

"She killed herself. Because of you! And you didn't even know about it."

"No, I was on a mission. I was at a retreat. I…"

"Retreat from this you worthless piece of shit."

I fall back as she slams the door in my face.

"I'll get her back," I cry, stumbling through the rose bushes, flailing my arms as thorns prick my skin.

But it didn't really happen like that.

***

I am alone on a dark stage, utterly confused, and looking out for what will happen next.

The Wicked Old Witch comes screaming in my face. "You are the Devil! You are the Devil!"

She claws at my skin, forces her thumbs into my mouth and rips into my cheeks with her thumbnails.

Her own face is covered with that clammy evil old lady sweat.

Lightning flashes left and right of her.

No matter how hard I try, I cannot talk. I cannot make any words come out of my mouth. I have no way to defend myself from this murderous witch.

But it didn't really happen like that.

***

It is nighttime at Psytron Headquarters.

Allison lifts a Petri dish for observation, "How can they be so dangerous?"

Regulator One tells her, "It is a form of life from another dimension, where evolution does not proceed on the physical plane."

She looks at all the scientific equipment and the other Petri dishes with snakes and slug-like creatures growing in them. Allison says, almost to herself, "Bloodsucking slugs crawling across dimensions? And with psychic powers?"

Elizabeth corrects her, "Psychotronic powers."

Regulator One says, "And yes, it is the perfect weapon. You just have to insert it correctly."

Allison is incredulous, "In the President's butt?"

Elizabeth says, "Don't be silly!"

Regulator One says, "In the Sleeper. He's pre-programmed to attack the President."

Allison is relieved. "In the Sleeper, yes of course."

Elizabeth explains, "It'll auto-activate, grow full size and then fly out at a preset proximity to the target."

Allison nods approvingly, and lets her eyes sparkle.

***

The Sleeper, nondescript anybody, is shot dead as soon as he steps out of a crowd on his way to the White House.

Vinney Cold Killer, top-secret man on the POTUS team, patiently gets down on one knee and takes new aim.

The snake rips through the air with jaws wide open, dripping venom, aiming straight for the President's neck. VCK calmly fires another shot, splattering psychotronic snakehead all over the place.

Then he simply secures his weapon, and walks away.

Mere pandemonium is not VCK's concern.

His job is done. The wheel has turned for all of us.

***

There is a dark stage in The Theater of the Absurd, with a backdrop presenting day-glow versions of the White House, the Hollywood Sign, and the Arch in Washington Square.

There is nothing else on the stage but one limp and ill-defined lump in the dark.

Allison is dead.

That is what I believe to be closest to the truth.

~12~

One More Night in Bangkok

We ain't in LA anymore.

It rains all the time, on and off, with wet heat you can never escape.

Then, THE DREAMER, an ostentatious, goofy-looking Japanese guru with a simian type Asian face, marches up to me at the temple gate.

I snap to attention.

I have been previously informed of his importance.

"You like images of the Buddha, Mr. Freeman?"

"Well Yes Sir, I certainly do."

"The Golden Buddha, the Emerald Buddha, you think we can learn anything looking at these lifeless statues day after day?"

"I ah…"

"Don't you want redemption for your sins?"

"Ah, well yes I…"

"Or do you want redemption from your own being?"

"Ah, you know, I'm not exactly sure what you mean when…"

"Mr. Freeman! The Universe is a machine for making deities."

There is a burst of warm rain. We ignore it.

"I, ah, I…"

"Do you know who said that?"

"I think you just did."

"Don't be a buffoon. It was a Frenchman, Henri Bergson. Don't you read French Mr. Freeman?"

"No, Sir. Sorry, I do not."

"I've been waiting a long time for your arrival. You can't hide your identity from me you know. Not from me."

Great, yeah, another guru knows more about me than I know about myself.

I don't say it, I just think it, but he hears it anyway.

He whispers into my ear, "I know all about your Black Magic too, and every secret you ever had."

I pull back, "Oh really?"

He scoffs at my purple bag. "And your books aren't going to help you here, not here, not anymore. We need our own Holy Trinity now. A Magic Triangle. You cannot use the head alone, and neither can I."

The Dreamer spins around on his heels, and I do my best to follow him.

We walk through a maze of Bangkok streets and dirt paths with shacks and huts. Occasionally, the smell of someone's dinner gives us a reprieve from the smell of garbage and waste.

There is abnormal anxiety. But I am somewhat comforted by the sight of children playing, and old ladies sitting outside, watching, oblivious to all the other problems in the world.

One bony and rickety old man sits in his room before a noisy old black-and-white TV, with his shirt off, waving a paper fan.

A baby cries all alone on a dirt floor.

What else is there? What could I expect to fill these rooms?

We eventually come to a shack at a dead-end.

The Dreamer points to a latch on a wooden shutter. I lift it. A frail OLD MONK in faded orange robes is working by candlelight. A pale young monk is sitting in the corner.

I try to talk, "We, ah, I and ah... we want, um..."

The Old Monk caresses the Buddha's Head in a polishing cloth, and motions for his visitors to enter the tiny room.

We enter and sit on the floor.

I stare at the pale monk in the corner, "Wai Yu?"

He doesn't answer.

I ask again, "Wai Yu?"

He says, "Why not me?"

I don't understand, "What?"

Wai Yu points right at me, leans forward and says, "Why you? That's the fucking question man!"

I say back, "I thought you were in LA, ya know, helping America or something."

"Fuck America man. I only went to LA to get you."

The Old Monk raises a hand, speaks softly, "The Perfect Buddha's Head is created from a sacred piece of Yew."

Oh no, that *you* problem again. I cannot avoid the question, "I don't really understand..."

Dreamer says, "Jesus was crucified on a cross of Yew too."

The Old Monk asks me, "Do you know why you are here?"

"Ah, Allison, I want..."

Wai Yu says, "Tell him who the fuck you are man."

"I… ah, I…"

Wai Yu says, "Don't you know who you are yet?"

The Dreamer sits up ramrod straight, announcing, "I will take the Perfect Buddha's Head now."

I am shocked at Wai Yu.

I am shocked at the Dreamer.

The Old Monk grabs the Head and holds it tight to his chest.

My heart sinks as the Perfect Buddha's Head is turned away from me.

I ask the Dreamer, "Why you?"

The air thickens as the Old Monk's face falls lifeless. Wai Yu jumps up, "Look! The old monk is in the Head!"

The Head is animate. It is alive. It is electric.

This is Real Magic. The Head turns and sees me sitting there, gross and oafish.

I talk to the Head. It seems somehow the thing I need to do, talk to the Head, but all I can say is, "I can't remember who I was, like just a minute ago! Or before that, who the fuck was I? Who am I now?"

The Head speaks, in a special voice:

"I am ONE.

All that is Real. All that is Unreal.

All that is, and is not.

I am undivided, and ONE."

This is blowing my mind, like really flipping me the fuck out!

The Head says, "This is who I am. This is what I know."

The Old Monk is perfectly still.

Even the Dreamer's slit-like narrow eyes are on fire. He reaches into his robe, pulls out a folded piece of dark silk, which, as he spreads it open on the floor, begins to look increasingly like a stained glass window, reflecting an undetectable source of light through its multicolored panels.

Then, he jumps up too, and delivers a sloppy roundhouse kick to the Old Monk's head, barely knocking over the frail and gentle man. But he does that thing with his lips, that exhalation noise, shaking his head fast, trying to look cool like Bruce Lee, the great Chinese Kung Fu Master himself.

Wai Yu and I watch helplessly as the Dreamer places the Head on his silk stained glass window.

Then he pulls the bag off my shoulder, and dumps out my books.

He deftly ties the corners of his wrapping cloth together, shoves the Head down tight into my bag, and throws it over his shoulder as he starts walking out.

~13~

Everything is Different

All I can do again is try to follow the Dreamer back on the same narrow paths, but now everything is different. The ground is too steep and slippery. The edges of things are too sharp.

There are no children playing. No old ladies. No one.

Snakes, slugs, slimy eels and other such freakish wormy creatures are swimming in the muddy paths and even in the dirty wet streets. I hear their disgusting splashing noises in the dark. I am terrified of touching them while I walk. They slam into me. They seem to be feeling me for something.

I am starting to understand more. This is their home. All of this belongs to them now, and I am the alien species.

The Dreamer keeps walking, and I keep walking behind him.

Finally, we reach a thick wall of moss-covered bricks. The Dreamer pulls a rusty handle, opens an iron slab, sticks his head in, pushes and pulls his bulky torso through the opening.

I follow, incapable of believing what I see, "What... Where is Bangkok?"

Half-bodies sit on damp sidewalks with hands outstretched, asking for money. Bodies with no hands or feet shove tin cans around to collect contributions, and use whatever stumps they have to guard their assets.

There are simply too many people everywhere you look.

"I just saw a head. A real head, just a head!"

A head without a face passes through the crowd.

Various kinds of snakes and slugs wiggle through the air in symmetry like schools of fish.

I am scared. I look down. Everything is dark and damp. "Is Bangkok salivating? Is it trying to swallow something?"

Giant cockroaches gnaw on human limbs.

I look away, unable to find respite in anything my environment can offer.

Young Thai boys come stick Sex Menus in my face.

Boy One says, "Any kind of boy, girl, or shemale will do anything you want."

I see Thai Solders stand proud, tough, and ready to enforce the rules. But what could the rules in this place possibly be?

It is all too bizarre.

I ask, "How does anyone know what you are supposed to do here?"

Boy Two says, "Sir, do you want a dream come true?"

"Am I being tested? Punished?"

Boy Three says, "You want a nightmare come true?"

The satisfaction on that soldier's face tells me everything is under control here, the way they want it.

Boy One steps back up into my face, "You have been warned, Mr. Free Man!"

I skip as carefully as possible over a dying man's thigh, chewed off at the knee, to follow the Dreamer as quickly as I can.

We reach the Chao Phraya River, hop on a waterbus, ride upstream past the Wat Arum Temple of Dawn and take a longboat taxi through the *klongs*, Bangkok's watery blood vessels.

We go farther and farther away from everything in the world I used to know.

We glide under a shaky bridge with savage guards.

I imagine dying with a spear in my back, and I wonder, is it better straight through the heart?

The Dreamer makes another announcement, "This is the place."

I feel eyes all around us. Evil human eyes, animal eyes, and demon eyes.

The Dreamer balances the wrapped-up Head on a mound of grass.

We sit in meditative poses on either side of the Head, illuminated with a beautifully multicolored Inner Light radiating through the silk wrapping.

The wrapping unties itself and slides down slowly.

The Dreamer motions for me to help him. We pick up The Perfect Buddha's Head together.

And then, I hear Allison calling, "Genetic... Genetic..."

I cry out, "Allison? Where are you? I'm not really crazy you know."

She says, "It was all a mistake."

Vague gasses and energies coagulate into visible forms.

She tells me, "After you die, existence is more complicated than when you are alive."

I'm just looking at her, staring, wanting her.

She says, "You think you know your own self, but who you are can vary greatly from who you think you have been."

"Oh God Allison..."

I cry. I beg. "I want you back. I want you back so much!"

She cannot accommodate my feelings.

There is no time or space for my emotions.

She continues, "People are standing shoulder-to-shoulder behind ordinary folding tables lined up on a huge stairway, clamoring for my attention, hooting and howling, like at a carnival sideshow, an incomprehensible cacophony."

Now I can say, "I see it. I see it."

Tables are arranged like this, on wide granite slab steps, leading up to something like a convention center complex.

Faces, caricatures, voices, all mixed up and confused.

Allison says, "I force myself to focus on one face, one voice."

It's a Girl.

The skin on her face is stretched inhumanly tight. Her teeth are exposed, chattering like a dummy's wooden teeth, lips drawn back in fixed smile.

Her wide dark eyes focus back on Allison.

She is seductive, "Come here, come here Allison."

She has beautiful hair, "It's me. It's me Allison."

The Girl pushes up against her side of the table.

"Yes, it's me Allison."

Allison says, "I see her milky-white breasts, like my own. Her softly rounded stomach."

The Girl whispers, "It's me Allison. It's me! Allison."

Allison breaths out, the girl breathes in.

The Girl's full red lips open, sucking in all the air.

Allison's lips pull all the way back, exposing all her teeth.

Allison, without lips, says, "What are you doing?"

The Girl swallows the breath from Allison's mouth like an elixir, like a magic potion, like the ultimate secret ingredient anyone could ever want.

Then she exhales, with a voice eerily like Allison's own, "It's me Allison. It's me. I'm Allison."

Allison is not breathing anymore.

"Yes, I'm Allison now. It's me..."

The Girl's words are reduced to the underlying flow of rhythmical but indistinguishable sound.

Buh dum, buh dum, buh dum.

She says, "You can feel the rhythm, but it is not yours anymore."

Buh dum, buh dum, buh dum.

Allison thinks she says, "I still exist, I think.

I think, therefore I am. Right?"

"Yes!" I say, "Yes!"

A wall of light self-illuminates into fluctuating waves of pink and powder blue. Particles fall to the floor, then disappear like incandescent snowflakes, leaving a path made of fairy dust, too magical to ignore. Allison steps on the powdery path and she is whooshed away at roller-coaster speed up into a cavernous space.

But the Girl tells her, "Wrong again."

"What?"

"You forgot about me."

"Who are you?"

Buh dum, buh dum, buh dum.

Allison says, "I feel the rhythm."

Buh dum, buh dum, buh dum.

"Are you God? *Ha Satan*! Are you the Devil?"

The Girl tells her, "Here and now, I am you."

Allison curls into a fetal position.

"I see myself float up to my own bosom, sucking for my own life."

"Yes, now think again pretty girl."

Allison says, "I can think, but I do not believe. I can think, therefore, I can doubt that I am!"

The Girl says, "Aha! You leave Descartes in the dust."

Allison keeps sucking, as her eyes grow blanker.

The Girl says, "Is that what you want? To become part of the undifferentiated energy randomly dispersed throughout the infinite cosmos?"

Allison cannot answer.

The Girl taunts her, "Yes, yes, yes. Come along now, my little Tinker Bell."

I scream.

"What are you doing?

Who are you?

Somebody's got her, somebody stole her damn soul!"

~14~

The Holy Conman

Hidden far away among the stars, there is a gravity-bending mass greater than 4 million of our suns, a super-massive black hole that gobbles up anything coming near it.

The Holy Conman made it, and it is his home.

His body is a perfect Astronomical Map of the cosmos. Each point of light is an entire world full of Cities of Angels. The most beautiful and complicated construction of light and energy anyone could ever imagine.

But at this particular place and time here in the Thai jungle, for reasons beyond my knowledge or control, sound waves blast into the brain of Genetic Freeman: "Your Body Is The Temple Of The Holy Ghost, Which Is In You, Which Ye Have Of God, And Ye Are Not Your Own."

The Operators, vast uncountable legions of Servile Spirits controlled by the Holy Conman, take over my body.

The world looks different as all my bodily systems are maximized.

Energy and flux. The original living complex of shapes and patterns. A light spectrum made to dazzle the gods. Sounds in a vibratory system reaching throughout all possible realms in conscious search of their own divine dissolution.

But then, fireballs of electricity crash into the ground. The Holy Conman's electromagnetic force field is jerked out in all directions. Someone is attacking the Holy Conman!

Operators try to avoid damage by contracting the Holy Conman's electrical field, but the Holy Conman is pinned down and stretched out like a butterfly on display.

There is a crackling noise and an urgent roar. Some operators try to fly through to launch a counter attack.

They burn up like moths in a volcanic flume.

~15~

The Lizard Lady's Lab

I am on a conveyor belt, moving past full-length mirrors, but I keep my eyes squeezed almost shut.

It feels like an assembly line in a large enclosed space, like an airplane hangar.

There are metal-on-metal noises, humming engines, spinning wheels.

I am terrified, but then I force myself to look, and in my peripheral vision I see an amorphous white mass attached to my body, like a hunchback.

I feel more attention focused on me than I ever imagined possible.

I look ahead. I am approaching the end of the line, where it exits through a hole in the wall.

I remember seeing Allison, and talking to her too. But that was somewhere else. I feel certain of her absence in this place.

Something is waiting for me. Someone is moving.

The line stops. The Lizard Lady is watching me from behind.

She has dozens of small clouds of luminous kaleidoscopic gas flying through silver-tinted air, like Tongues of Fire, making whooshing and whooping sounds as the clouds fly by and stabilize at destinations around the room.

I feel something touching the white mass on my back. I try to turn, but I can't move. I hear a sharp crack and feel a release of pressure, like from a lever being lifted.

I turn and see...

A nurse? A lizard? Marilyn Monroe?

It's a caricature of a female with green-and-black scaly hide, and a voluptuous bosom stuffed into a big white bra. And she is dressed, I think, like some kind of nurse or something.

I don't understand.

I reach out and shove one hand inside the V-top of her uniform, under her bra.

I really don't understand. But I feel reassured somehow, about something.

My hand is happy...

Until I look up and see a smug grin on her otherwise beautiful face, and she says, "Good boy."

I pull my limp empty hand away as inconspicuously as possible.

"I fell for the same trap again, didn't I?"

The Lizard Lady sing-songs to me like to a little baby, "Uh oh! Now you have to go into the Surrealistic Carnival of Total Demonic Control."

I am helplessly and hopelessly pulled ahead on the assembly line.

***

Now, I am the Speaker at Psytron Headquarters under a big picture of Regulator One.

And I am more confused than anyone how this came to be.

Slick Willie walks in escorting a shuffling old Japanese Clown with one eye and a bad leg.

The Clown is holding a measuring stick, with a set of false teeth on top, and a string hanging down from the bottom jaw.

Willie pushes him toward me in the Lecture Room, "Here, I caught him joking on some *gaijin* on the *Yamanote Line.*"

I tell Willie, "Something's wrong man. I'm in LA, ya know. A *gaijin* is a foreigner in Japan. The *Yamanote Line* is a train in Tokyo… And I do not know how I know that."

"We ain't kids anymore Free Man. Things ain't like ya thought, ya know."

"Okay, okay, but he's cool Willie. He's good people."

The Clown is visibly relieved. He thanks me.

"*Doumo arigatou, Mr. Robotto.*"

I think he is happy.

But then he stands up in his shabby clown suit, pulls me over, picks me up, and throws me out onto the street like garbage, in the middle of Tokyo.

Slick Willie looks like he knew it would happen, just like that.

He gives me the peace sign, bidding his unfortunate friend farewell.

✷✷✷

I get up off the ground and hurry toward a group of American Sailors talking to some young Japanese girls in the middle of the street.

I tell them, "I am a special agent sent by the President of the United States to ascertain the mental health of American citizens in Japan."

Everyone vanishes before my eyes.

I look around, not sure what to do. I walk. I wander down into an empty train station.

I see mysterious figures at the end of the platform, leaning against the wall, waiting for something on the other side of an imposing ticket gate.

A leather-ish Dyke and her two Shemale lovers.

They are all armed with automatic weapons and police-type belts with handcuffs, dildos, sex toys.

I ask, "Uhm, are we waiting for something here?"

The Dyke raises her weapon at me, "Step away from the bars please."

The Shemales raise their weapons at me too.

I start backing away, giving the peace sign.

"Hey, be cool. Peace, that's all I want."

The Dyke says, "Sure, everyone just wants a piece. And when all the pieces are gone, what's left? Huh? Tell me wise guy, what's left? Huh? An empty hole is all!"

"I... I'm..."

The Dyke says, "That's far enough you carny freak."

I stop.

Shemale Won says, "Most people think nothing comes here but the train."

Shemale Too says, "Yeah, but you like to come here, don't you?"

I look around.

The Dyke says, "Don't bother looking for a way out."

I look again.

They all aim their weapons, ready to fire.

"You have been warned Mr. Free Man!"

There are no bars behind me, that is the way I came in.

I turn, run fast as I can. They fire and miss. I escape up the stairs and back out onto the street.

✳✳✳

Bar hostesses are getting off work.

A drunken salaryman bends over to throw up in the gutter, and a friend pats him on the back to comfort him.

That is the way it works here late at night.

But the rest of this I simply cannot explain.

A half-naked Old Lady comes running up the street toward me, animated and noisy, but incoherent.

I say, "I'm sorry *Obaasan*, do I know you?"

Her skin is wrinkled and sagging. Eyes bulging.

She starts pulling on her own unusually long nipples. Pulling her exhausted old tits way harder than anyone expects.

I try to look away, try to leave, but a crowd forms around the Old Lady and me.

A young Hostess steps forward, gets on one knee, opens her blouse, pulls out her own leathery nipples, preposterously longer than the Old Lady's, almost like dicks.

The Hostess starts to stroke and squeeze those big beefy nipples until she forces out a stream of strange liquid that squirts out to collect in a puddle on the already damp ground in front of the silent crowd.

I really can't tell anymore if she has nipples or dicks in her hands. And I can't tell what the liquid is.

Milk? Sperm? Blood? What the hell is it?

She squeezes it out in spasms, without comment from anyone.

Then she lifts one hand and catches a line from the weakening stream on the back of her fingers.

From the way it bridges the spaces between her fingers, it has the thick sticky consistency of male ejaculate.

She lifts her hand closer to her face and says, "*Kusai, kore wa.* This stinks."

Perhaps it is malodorous...

But her faux disapproval turns to a deliciously naughty grin.

She is quite proud of herself.

"How do I know? How do I know what she says?"

I dissolve into the collection of moisture left on the street and disappear from the scene, down into the ground.

I feel unknown hands tug on my ankles, pulling me down deeper and deeper into the dark earth.

"This is not my place. This is not my problem."

I am bound to a post. Not who I just was, and maybe not who I think I am. But who I used to be.

I plead, "I don't understand. I'm just an old lady. Why do you need to burn me? Why are you killing me like this?"

Flames race up all around my body.

"You are the same fools that burn me every time!"

Thunderous laughter reverberates all around me.

"I try not to hate you, but I do hate you, I hate you to death!"

A swarm of demons engulfs me and carries me away.

I scream at the fools burning me, "Even though my eyes steam and melt, I know you will suffer more than I."

The demon swarm grows limitless, thickens into an ocean of tar-like slime, mocking me with insane laughter and crying, "Help me. Help me."

I cry out at them too, "I hear you! I hear you!"

There is wave after wave of laughing and crying.

"Help me. Help me."

"I'm sorry, I don't know what to do."

"Help me. Help me."

What can cause this much horror?

The Universe answers with a distant movement of something so massive it is like a shift in the position of the sun.

"Oh God. No. I'm sorry. I don't want to know anything at all anymore. I'm sorry I ever did. Please God, let me just negate myself."

I am beaten and afraid.

"Obliterate me like I never existed. You don't need me. I don't want to be here anymore. God, please..."

✳✳✳

The Lizard Lady walks to the end of the assembly line, where I am still waiting with my eyes squeezed shut again.

The clouds of colored gas whoosh around her, and whoop, whoop to a stop.

She tells me, "Don't be silly Genetic. You cannot simply negate your own existence."

I open my eyes, thoroughly exhausted, and say,

"In the Old Testament, Job suffers for seven days and begs God not merely to die, but to have never been born."

She says, "If there is one thing we know from the Israelites covenant with God, you cannot escape from God."

My body pushes through the exit into an all-encompassing electromagnetic field.

***

And in the Thai jungle…

The Holy Conman directs a positive pulse of operators in a laser-sharp energy flow. Hits a negative vibration in the electromagnetic containment shield, and shoots through the hole.

An all-encompassing voice demands to know:

"Who are you?"

There is an ear-piercing implosion.

The shield disintegrates.

One body is left burned and bleeding, face down in the mud.

***

I wake up in the middle of the night, huddled in the grass. I smell the dankness of my own blood.

I force myself to get up.

I float and paddle all the dark and winding wet way back to the hotel's riverside entrance.

I climb up onto land just as the Sun is rising and the rivers are coming alive with all the myriad activities of the ancient mercantile and pedestrian interests of the citizens of Bangkok.

~16~

Bad to Worse

Three slightly built, pink-robed Virgins, in identical Dreamer masks, surround me, and stare at me.

The Dreamer waves his fingers and speaks without looking up, "You are becoming an increasingly curious character."

The Virgins leave.

The Dreamer turns to face me.

"Who are you Mr. Genetic Free Man?"

I say, "What are you talking about?"

He says, "Don't you know? Don't you even know who you are?"

"It's me! You just said, you just called me..."

I stumble over to a full-length mirror.

"Holy Mother of God. It is not me."

I wipe blood and filth off my face.

"I'm not me. I'm not who I am."

I look closer.

"I'm insane."

"I mean, I always thought I was insane. But now I finally understand... I am really insane."

The Dreamer says, "What happened out there?"

I say, "I don't care. I can't care about the unthinkable things anymore. I give up."

The Dreamer tells me, "Yeah, you're a pussy."

✳✳✳

Everything is just too fucked up.

I collapse face-first on the bed.

✳✳✳

I see Allison walk into a large formal cocktail reception. The Staff are dressed in black-and-white uniforms, carrying trays of champagne glasses filled with a greenish liquid.

Allison scans the crowd. I follow her gaze from across the room to a lady with outrageous patchwork skin, like a metallic quilt of blue, gray, and silver.

Allison can't believe her eyes but she doesn't want to attract attention to herself. She walks toward me, pointing urgently at that lady, as if she came here specifically to tell me about her because no one else will tell me what I need to know. She expects to look at me face-to-face, but now I am lying on the floor.

She bends down to touch my shoulder, I turn face-up, but there is no face on the front of my head. My legs are gone. I have a scaly tail, like a fish or reptile. It is the same scaly patchwork as that lady she is trying to warn me about.

I flip my tail up in the air. She sees my face, serene, on the underside of my tail flap. I show no emotion, no desire, and no expression of recognition at all.

The outrageous Patchwork Lady comes over and starts sticking acupuncture needles inside small white circles almost hidden in the pattern of my own patchwork skin.

She grabs a glass full of the green liquid, hands it to me. I drink it while she connects the needles to wires on a bizarre electronic device. She turns a lever, and electricity flows into me through a multi-colored electromagnetic field.

Allison retreats.

She doesn't know what to do here anymore.

***

The Witch is on her Throne in the Gypsy Room, occupied with her own magical affairs, manipulating her mysterious equipment, her crystals, Tarot Cards, Ouija Board.

She says, "The ancient Egyptians understood that one great danger in the afterlife is traveling through the underworld upside down."

She looks up with fiery green eyes to warn us all.

"If you get stuck upside down, you end up eating your own excrement for the rest of eternity."

She enjoys a malevolent laugh.

"Although it is wise to know techniques to avoid this predicament...

Today this knowledge is rare."

***

Demon warriors occupy the Dreamer's hotel room while he and I are asleep. Hoards of parasitic and cannibalistic devils.

The Dreamer feels a voodoo doll clasped in his own hand, under his pillow. He is shocked into a consciously vivid dreaming state, being judged by a jury of twelve translucent white zombies in a trial presided over by Baron Samedi, Lord of the Graveyard.

The Dreamer sees his room is full of prohibited pornographic materials and illegal sex toys. He knows the hidden things are there. Stone containers of ancient ointments and salves for compounding the Witches' Ungent.

He knows his sanity and his life are at stake.

I am corralled in with dozens of other Prisoners and Slaves being forced to act out scenes depicted in the prohibited pornographic materials.

The Baron watches, with his left hand on the judicial gavel and his right hand under his black robes, slowly and patiently stroking his penis up and down.

He does this at a pace that could only be maintained by an impartial arbiter of guilt and innocence. His manner and deportment are otherwise and in all ways appropriate and befitting to the high office of Judge.

Unfortunately, the Prisoners and Slaves simply cannot complete the scenes.

There is panic in a young girl's eyes as she refuses further participation and explodes out from the stomach.

***

The Wicked Old Witch watches from her Throne.

She approves of what she sees.

"Masterful manipulation of the human instinct for self-preservation."

She takes delicious delight in the situation.

"Fear is so great, there is no time to think anything except: Do this or die."

She smiles, "Then, after you have already been manipulated into doing things you would rather die than do…"

She savors this the most. The words, the idea, they cause her to tremble with joy.

"The death you are finally forced to accept is filled with shame."

She feels a thrill tingle all through her body.

She waves her hand through the smoke and fog of her room.

A vision appears, Hermes Trismegistus, the greatest magician and king that ever lived, writes on a scroll in the Library of Alexandria:

"As it is Above, so it is Below."

Genetic hears it, repeats it to himself:

"As it is Above, so it is Below."

The Wicked Old Witch says, "It doesn't matter.

He doesn't know how to use it here.

He doesn't know what it means now."

~17~

Prisoners & Slaves

Prisoners and Slaves are kept in a labyrinth of individual cells and caves. There are iron bars and heavy wooden doors in underground catacombs carved out of solid rock to keep the dead detained forever, far away from the living.

Chariots with iron-rimmed wooden wheels ride on cobbled stone roads. The male charioteers carry black leather whips and heavy iron shields.

People are in strange costumes, like early American pilgrims, pirates and witches.

There are white-coated medical technicians, mirror-faced astronauts, blue-suited, fast-walking and fast-talking businessmen.

Time is all messed up, but no matter, it is already too late.

The perpetrators march into the courtyard confident and in control. A group of female warriors leads the way for a thundering, wildly adorned Savage Priestess carrying a crescent-shaped sickle.

She stands almost twenty feet tall, the Aztec Goddess of Illicit Passion, Lust and Filth. Her name is Tlazolteotl, but no one dares even whisper it.

Everyone is sprinkled with colored powder that is claimed to be the Devil's sperm. Animals, men and women of all irregular shapes, sizes and colors begin to copulate with a hellish frenzy.

Double agents and spies are leaving the ranks of both the prisoners and the guards to join the triumphant tribal parade.

An elderly female prisoner steps forward with a freakish smile and rotten teeth. She reaches out for a coconut shell cup, sucks it dry and wipes her mouth with her forearm.

A crowd forms around her. She steps into a hollow cradle made from tree bark tied around thin branches. She climbs in and lies down on her back, face up to the crowd.

Music grows frantic, tribal drumming with other screaming and screeching instruments.

People sprinkle the prostrate lady with more colored powders.

The High Priestess squats at the foot-end of the cradle, opens her knees and sprays out a steaming yellow stream.

The warriors hack at the cradle and its occupant with machetes and spears.

Blood and urine roll down to the woman's face.

She is dying with a frozen smile, more relaxed and subtle now, like the Mona Lisa, like beatnik Joan.

The Goddess bends forward to lift the woman's head into her oversize mouth and begins to ingest her the way a snake devours a mouse. She swallows, gobbles and sucks the victim in, deeper and deeper, one gulp at a time, until the feet finally flap farewell to all the astonished faces.

The music stops.

No one makes a sound.

No one takes a breath.

The Goddess grunts.

She scrunches.

She gives a deep sigh of relief, and we see her deposit an even more wasted version of the female victim, head first, back into the cradle.

After an unpleasant pause, the devoured and digested woman rises, slobbering words of gratitude as she crawls down to grovel at the Goddess's feet, in a puddle of her own unnatural afterbirth.

No one else gets up to join the tribe.

I have no one to talk to, no way to review what I have seen. Clearly, alienation is part of the plan.

I am too exhausted to close my own mouth.

I am wondering only one thing: Why can't it just end?

Please, I can't take it anymore.

~18~

Only You

My body is removed to center stage in a dark theater.

Lights come on.

There is a Japanese *seppuku* ritual self-disembowelment by sharp short knife.

Then, a Samurai cuts off the entire head with one swing of a razor-sharp long sword.

I see my own neck with skin like a raw chicken.

I feel the head being cut off, but I do not die.

Teeth grow at the rim, and they make the neck cavity into a big wet mouth.

A blood-gorged penis rises up inside the neck from where a chicken-skin sack strains at the weight of two heavy balls.

The teething neck bites down tight on this protruding shaft, chewing and struggling until it rips the tip right off.

The severed end falls flat on the floor.

Beautiful, seductive fingers pick it up, and hold the severed piece in front of the neck as if eyes were there to see it.

The balls spin round and focus as if with gyroscopic powers.

The fingers return the severed piece, feeding it tip down, so the neck can take another bite.

I hear Allison say, "You and I are the only ones who belong here."

"Allison?"

I hear her again. "You and I are the only ones who can endure this."

"Oh my God Allison, how did you end up here?"

She says, "I needed to be somewhere only you could find me."

Part Five:
In The Eastern Capital

19. The Dreamer

20. The English Teacher

21. Peach, Knife, Eel

22. What Is Love?

23. Revolution

24. Violence

25. Freedom

Anthony Lojac

~19~

The Dreamer

The Three Virgins dress me like the Bizarro version of David Bowie and the alien rock-god, Ziggy Stardust. I look far from normal, but nowhere near as glamorous as Ziggy either.

They escort me into a room, in their Dreamer masks, with sublime frozen smiles.

The Dreamer is sitting with tea service for two. He is calm, actually quite beatific here in his own element.

I must say however, my own face feels frighteningly insane.

I am afraid I am not cool anymore.

I look for a mirror, rubbing my hands up and down my outfit, "This doesn't feel right."

The Dreamer says, "You don't remember do you?"

The Virgins giggle. Pointing at me, touching my clothes and my body.

"I'm not sure if I forgot, or if I remember, or if I'll ever remember to think about what I forgot again."

Virgin One says, "Is that English?"

Virgin Two says, "I remember to think I forget."

Virgin Three says, "I forgot to think I don't remember!"

The Virgins continue giggling.

The Dreamer says, "We cannot let the hungry demons find you again, or they will eat you alive and excrete you like human waste."

Virgin One says, "Ewww. *Gross* me out."

Virgin Two says, "Gross me *out!*"

Virgin Three says, "Gross *me* out!"

I say, "Yeah, let's not do that okay? We don't need to gross *anyone* out."

Dreamer waves his fingers.

He says, "Demons are not all bad. The word demon actually means replete with wisdom."

I say, "Okay, yeah, far out man."

The Virgins serve tea.

He says to me, "Why don't you Americans know what your own words mean?"

"I don't really…"

"A good demon is called an Eudemon. A bad demon is a Cacodemon."

"Yeah, okay."

"You were trapped by the lowest filth-loving devils."

The Three Virgins tell me, "You are a bad boy! Bad. Bad. Bad."

"I'm sorry. I don't know what to say…"

Dreamer waves his hand in disgust.

"I made this tea for you. Drink it. Become more like me. More like God."

"What can I say? I'm sorry…"

"Shut up, and drink tea."

The Virgins tell me again, "You are a bad boy! Bad. Bad. Bad Boy!"

I shut my mouth, swallow before I even drink or speak.

"Thank you Dreamer. Yes, maybe I should be more like you."

The Virgins say, "More like God!"

"Thank you Dreamer, yes, you make me more like God, please."

I drink the tea. It smells strange, but I drink it.

The Dreamer waves his fingers again, announces, "Mask Off!"

I check my face.

The Virgins take off their masks.

Their eyes are on the tea.

I am taken aback. They are pure and lovely.

The Dreamer warns me, "The Virgins will take care of you. But you better be careful."

"Okay, yeah... Careful?"

"Illicit sex is not allowed here."

"Really? No sex here?"

"Not for you! Not even a single masturbatory fantasy will go unpunished."

"I understand. Yes Sir! *Kashikomarimashita!*"

Virgin One asks the other girls, "Is that Japanese?"

Virgin Two says, "I forgot. *Wasureta.*"

Virgin Three says, "I can't remember. *Oboerarenai.*"

The Virgins continue giggling.

The Dreamer continues educating me into his strange and increasingly dangerous world. "The human imagination, excited by lust and lewd fantasies, secretes a non-corporeal sperm."

I say nothing.

He pushes, "Do you know that?"

I see images of sperm ghosts floating through the air, and I say, "Ah, no, I never heard of non-corporeal sperm before."

Virgin One says, "What kind of what, are they talking about?"

Virgin Two says, "Non-corporeal..."

Virgin Three says, "Sperm! Non-corporeal sperm."

The Dreamer explains, "Male and female demons, Incubi and Succubi, are born from ejaculations of the onanistic imagination."

I hesitate, but I do ask, "So you mean, I make demons from my ghost sperm?"

The Virgins say to each other, "Boys are so stupid... And dirty too!"

The Dreamer tells me "Yes, that is correct."

I say, "That's, ah, pretty heavy, I guess."

He says, "Then I'd have to remove your penis."

The Virgins all put hands to mouth in mock shock.

"You say what? Um, I'm not sure what you said, or what you mean, but my penis is not the removable kind you know."

The Dreamer is serious.

"I can help you Mr. Freeman. But you must help me too."

"Yeah, yeah, I'll help you, okay, and we leave my penis exactly where it is."

"Your Bible says Jesus went into the wilderness alone for forty days to test himself in the struggle between Good and Evil."

"I don't think I understand..."

"Then, shut up and listen."

"Yes Sir."

"When Jesus returns, he sees a man possessed by an evil spirit."

The Virgins wave their arms as if casting out a demon, "Be silent, and come out of him!"

The Dreamer waves his arms around with even more drama and says, "Jesus casts out the demon!"

Then, after a short awkward silence, I try to straighten up a bit and say, "May I ask, I mean, about me? Like, why am I here?"

The Dreamer's attitude grows past pride and arrogance to malice and domination as he sees me so pathetic.

He warns me, "You have a great capacity to absorb the bad Karma of those around you."

I'm thinking hard, real hard. But that sneaky guy at the Honolulu airport was right. There is a lot more to life than one equals one.

I say, "I have a really big problem here now. Don't I?"

The Dreamer is perfectly satisfied.

~20~

The English Teacher

It takes a few years, but eventually, I think I'm healthy again.

I do what the Dreamer says. I am obedient.

I am shorthair Genetic now. I wear the proper uniform for my time and place, the ubiquitous blue suit of the Japanese salaryman.

The Dreamer approves, "I'm impressed. You have finally learned to act like a man."

"Yes Sir, I feel pretty good about acting like myself, Sir!"

"You may use the phone now too, for English practice with your girls."

"My girls? Ah, Now I have girls?"

"You will be teaching English to a whole class full of girls. You will recruit new members for me."

"I teach English, and I recruit new members. Okay. And I have girls? Yes very nice, I have girls."

The Dreamer shakes his head at how idiotic I still am, "You bring the girls to me. Do you understand?"

"Right, right, yes, bring the girls to you, yes of course."

***

I walk into a class full of giggling fresh faces.

I say, "Good morning young ladies."

All the girls, except one rocker type in the back row, smile and greet their new teacher in sing-songy English, "Goo morning Ge-ne-ric Sensei."

SAYAKO sits there in back with unmoving black eyes.

"Genetic," I say loud enough for the entire class, Ge-ne-tic!"

The girls stare at my mouth, all the way from my lips to my teeth, tongue and throat, and giggle even more at my strange pronunciation.

Sayako smiles slightly.

***

Then, one cold and windy evening, later in the school year, I escort that intriguing young lady from the back row of my class into the Dreamer's room.

"Dreamer, this is Sayako…"

He immediately tells me, "You may leave, Sensei."

I say, "Sayako is…"

She says, "You may leave now, Teacher."

She tells the Dreamer who she is by herself.

"I am Sayako!"

He tells her, "Please, have some tea."

I bow obediently.

And as I back out of the room, I see how Sayako smiles more at this humble version of her English teacher.

~21~

Peach, Knife, Eel

Sayako is in her bed, in a two-piece pink nightie.

There is a sharp steel knife showing on a strip of her naked stomach.

She is playing with her fingers in her pubic hair.

Speaking into a phone at her ear with her left hand, she asks me, "Do you like *kuroge*?"

I'm on the phone at my table, sitting on my knees on the *tatami* floor.

I say, "I'm sorry?"

She says, "My shiny black hair, do you like it?"

"Yeah, of course, it's beautiful."

"You like *kuroge* more than *kinpatsu*?"

I try to remember. I think. "That's blond right?"

But I think too slowly for her.

She grabs a peach, at her side.

"Do you like peach?"

"Ah, you mean peach color hair?"

"Do you like peach? It is simple question."

She cuts the peach in half, dripping onto her chest.

"Okay, yes, yes I like peach."

"Your English is problem."

She gently touches the tip of her nipple with the juicy wet pit still in the peach.

I mumble, "Yeah..."

Sayako smiles, removes the pit.

I'm quiet.

She rubs both halves juicy-side down on her little titties.

"Peach is like two sweet wet mouths sucking on my *chichi kubi*."

I exhale.

Then she moves the peaches around, kissing her body in good places, until she hears squishing sounds from the spastic motion of her own hands.

A muscle in her forearm starts to ache, and she collapses from one sweaty convulsion after another.

When Sayako relaxes back in bed, she is looking at tentacle sex pictures in her art book, "Do you know Shunga?"

"Ah, Japanese erotic art?"

"Do you know famous Japanese artist name Hokusai? Dream of the Fisherman's Wife? Two octopus, kiss nipples and pussy."

"I do know it actually, yes."

Sayako is amused. She shakes her head and says, "Sometimes I think, maybe I go to fish market for eel. I ask Fishmonger, 'May I have a big fat one please?' "

The Fishmonger gives young Sayako a vigorously flip flopping eel she carries home in a clear plastic bag.

She takes the slimy thing out, lays it on a chopping board, and shoves an ice pick into its eye.

Then she squats above the wagging tail, and allows it to be her lover.

She says, "It is *ikenai*. Bad. Dirty…

So I want to do it more. I like *ikenai*."

I say, "You tell me things no one else ever talks about."

Her eyes sparkle mischievously.

She says again, "I like *ikenai*."

✷✷✷

And then…

One day, Sayako is in her school uniform shopping with Mother.

The Fishmonger greets them. "The eels are very sweet this time of year, aren't they young lady?"

Mother is clueless.

Sayako confesses with tears streaming down her cheeks, "I try to cook eel for Honorable Father. But I fail, and throw out every time. I so ashamed."

Her mother decides to instruct Sayako in the intricate process of cleaning, marinating and grilling fresh eel.

She tells the Fishmonger, "Please give us your best eel today."

The Fishmonger grabs the biggest, thickest eel, slides the thing into a clear plastic bag and hands it to Sayako to carry home, same as always.

"Here is a nice big fat one for Honorable Young Daughter."

***

Mother and Sayako arrive home from market.

Mother opens the bag, takes out the eel, sticks the pick into its eye and fixes it to the board.

She cuts from base of neck to end of tail while the body is still trying to wiggle away.

She instructs her daughter, "You must keep the sharp edge against the backbone all the way."

They remove the internal organs and keep the liver for soup. They wash the eel. Cut off the head, tail and fins. Insert five wooden skewers equidistant from top to bottom.

"It is best grilled over a charcoal fire, but gas or electric is okay too."

They cook it over a gas grill.

Sayako asks, "Three minutes each side?"

"Yes, three minutes each side. Rinse to remove excess fat. Brush with sweet sauce. And grill one more minute each side."

"Then finished?"

Her mother says, "No, no, no! You must repeat entire sequence three times."

She's got it, "Three is the magic number!"

They do it three times.

"Now we cut into ten-centimeter pieces and lay it on top of sticky white rice."

They garnish each bowl with pickled ginger, and a sprinkle of *sansho*, special Japanese ground pepper.

They sit and sip aromatic Japanese Ocha while they eat.

Honorable Daughter says, "I had no idea eel tasted so good!"

Mother is happy.

"Wild eels are better because the meat is tender and sweet as the finest French pâté."

Sayako is happy.

"I like the big fat ones a lot."

***

I listen to her story.

I learn about her, her family, and her eels.

I go, "Wow!"

Wow, wow, wow, wow, wow.

She says, "Now Honorable Father proud I love him and cook eel for him all by myself."

I say, "You know, in the eighth circle of the Inferno in Dante's Divine Comedy, there is a ditch full of pitiful souls constantly bitten by serpents."

She says, "Oh yeah?"

I tell her, "Then the serpents mutate into the person they have just bitten, and the bitten person mutates into a serpent, ad infinitum."

"They both eat each other forever?"

"Forever."

"Cool!"

Yeah, I knew for sure she'd like that a lot.

~22~

What is Love?

On the last day of class, the quiet girl in the back row uncharacteristically raises her hand.

I acknowledge her as I start passing out exam papers.

She says, "May we discuss a short quote?"

"Why yes, of course, ah, Sayako right? But this is the final..."

"You know our school motto, 'Love God and Serve His Chosen People.'"

"Yes, yes I know but..."

She says, "Teach me, how can I love God?"

"I... ah... That's a very good question Sayako. But you should ask someone else about your school motto, the principal perhaps? I don't really know…"

"But I want to know what love is."

"Young lady, we all want to know what love is!"

She says, "I found a quote from the French poet, Charles Pierre Baudelaire."

"Oh?"

Sayako unhesitatingly reads aloud.

"The supreme voluptuous delight of love lies in the certainty of doing evil."

I proceed in a daze.

"Okay let's just do the final, okay?"

~23~

Revolution

I have one last mission. I'm in a bank, undercover, marching down the hall as a highly paid Wall Street Expat.

I step into a conference room full of Revolutionary Comrades. The Chief is telling everyone, "Chairman Mao said the basis for guerrilla discipline must be the individual conscience. With guerrillas, a discipline of coercion is ineffective."

I awkwardly try to find a place in the group. "Sounds like I'm in the right place. Theatrical Psychic Terrorists, right? The Volunteers of Japan? Or something like that?"

The Chief clarifies, "We are attacking The Man and his merciless, monolithic, materialistic political-economic machine by robbing one of its biggest banks. Is that what you mean?"

I remember exactly what the Dreamer told me, 'You steal all the yen cash from the terrorists, and re-route it into my secret account.'

I say, "Yes! That is exactly what I mean."

The Chief is not impressed, "Asshole."

I think, maybe I gotta get outta this place while I still can.

But then, Sayako appears on the scene.

She looks like a rock star, with some kind of angry young Japanese guy at her side.

She announces her own arrival, "Ta, da...!"

The Angry Guy says, "Hey suit, we are psychic terrorists, remember? We can hear your stupid ideas inside your head, you know?"

Sayako is not done with her self-introduction.

"I am, I am, Sayako Kuroge!

Japanese artist!

And I have no guilt!"

Yeah, I remember, all about *kuroge*.

The Angry Guy tells me, "Just because you're white-meat you think you got some special right to extricate yourself from this nightmare and leave Japan a healthy and wealthy guy?"

I try to act like I don't know Sayako.

In fact, I caution myself, I do not even know if Sayako is working undercover for the Dreamer, or not.

She looks at me, and thinks to herself, "I don't even know if he has one of those psychotronic snakes stuffed up his butt, or not."

The Angry Guy yells, "All my brothers packin'?"

Nobody is packing. Nobody understands.

But they all chip in.

"Power to the people!"

"Right on!"

"Off the pig!"

I tell the Angry Guy, "My mind always drifts at these meetings, but I just have to look good anyway, right?"

He says, "Who the fuck says you look good?"

I don't really enjoy trying to talk to that guy.

I nonchalantly lean toward Sayako and listen to her chatter with the Comrades sniffing around her ass.

There are several of them, literally sniffing around her ass.

She tells them, "I am lead singer for 'God's Pussy.' "

Chief gets excited, "I love God's Pussy!"

Sayako tells him, "Everyone loves God's Pussy."

She turns, looks directly at me.

"Ah, yeah, me too, sure I love God's Pussy, yeah, it's great." I look away, and try to avoid further direct talk with Sayako.

She doesn't let me go.

She's up in my face again, "Do you like black hair?"

I look back and say, "Yes, yes I do like black hair."

She stands, stretches seductively. The butt-sniffers follow close, tongues wagging like dogs.

I watch her, but I feel something strange on my skin. I nervously touch my face, and find a slug crawling on my cheek.

I wonder why no one has told me about it. I mean how can you not tell someone about a snake crawling on their face?

I try to brush it off, but it attaches more securely. I grab it, tug hard, rip it off, bunch the thing into a ball and hold it for further observation.

The Chief explains, "We have occupied rooms on the 36th floor and hacked into the security network. We will execute a series of explosions on other floors and conduct the robbery during the ensuing pandemonium."

Sayako's Angry Guy smirks to the comrade next to him because I obviously can't understand anything.

They all go, "Right on! Power to the people! Off the pig!"

The Angry Guy says, "We'll steal a fortune, and do a shit-load of political damage too!"

I risk saying, "Ah, let me just inquire, please, I mean, why is it taking so long?"

He says, "What the hell is wrong with you man? Shut the fuck up!"

Sayako suddenly comes over and pulls my face to her bosom for a hug.

"You miss me, don't you?"

"Huh?"

The butt-sniffers scatter out of her way.

"You know what I mean."

"No, no, I don't know what you are talking about, not at all."

Comrades cackle and sneer.

The Chief spits out at me, "You know you want it."

The Angry Guy says, "Why does he get it anyway, this foreign pig?"

Sayako laughs a little.

Then she kisses my neck and mouth, slowly, luxuriously and lovingly.

I feel her hug tighter and start grinding up and down on my leg.

I keep my thigh muscle tense and grind back up into her warm crotch nice and hard.

The Comrades slap their own thighs, laughing out of control.

Snakes are winding around her ankles and calves, crawling up her legs.

I feel the creatures start climbing onto me too. But I keep making out with Sayako, working my tongue along her lips, down her neck and onto her chest, while I try to push the creepy crawlers off my skin.

I think, maybe now I know where these things come from.

But the snakes don't seem to bother Sayako at all.

She grabs the back of my head, humps and grinds herself against me even tighter and faster.

When she finally cries out loud, it is with utter abandon for everyone to hear. "Oh God yes. I love it! I love it!"

No one else dares breathe a word.

And then, she is perfectly still.

I stand there.

I look at her.

She is lovely.

Her thighs are smooth and beautiful. There are no slugs, no snakes crawling up her legs.

I say, "I wonder, do you love it because you love it? Or do you love it because everyone is watching you, and laughing at me?"

***

The Wicked Old Witch observes everything from her Magic Throne.

"He dreamt of Sayako and her pretty little pussy so many times, but it wasn't like this. No, it was not like this... Nothing is like he expected."

***

I feel the slug in my pocket.

I've got to do something about it.

I say, "I have to reconnoiter at another rendezvous point."

I shuffle backwards out the door, and walk away at the same brisk pace as the other blue suits.

***

The Chief says, "Who is that guy anyway?"

The Angry Guy says, "What is he here for?"

Chief asks, "We got a use for him, haven't we?"

Sayako says, "Yes, he fills a need."

Angry Guy says, "All I see him fill is your hole."

Sayako snaps back, "Somebody's got to do it."

He says, "Yeah, right."

Comrades laugh, like robots, "Ha. Ha. Ha. Ha."

Angry Guy says, "He thinks he can fool us into thinking he is so cool, but he is just a stupid animal."

The Chief says, "His problem is he doesn't know what he knows and he doesn't want us to know he doesn't know."

"Dude, like who cares who the fuck he is or what the fuck he thinks he knows anyway?"

"That's what I mean. He cares a lot because people are watching him."

"Hey, did you see that fucking *hebi* go to work on his face?"

"That was a snake?"

"Who couldn't see it man? Look like baby Godzilla climbing up and down his dumb ass face."

Sayako laughs like a robot too, "Ha. Ha. Ha. Ha."

Chief asks, "Did he eat it?"

Angry Guy says, "No, he didn't eat it, he keeps it in his pocket or something."

Sayako laughs again, "Ha. Ha. Ha. Ha."

~24~

Violence

Late one particularly creepy night, after I had already gone to sleep, I am called in to drink tea with the Dreamer.

We sit in front of his altar to Shiva, the Hindu god of destruction, and Kali, Shiva's frightening mother and lover.

The Dreamer is in his dark royal kimono and blood red robe under. He is burning incense and playing the eerie music he likes.

I say, "Kali is your favorite."

He says, "Why does she rip off the head of her lover? Why does she eat the children to whom she gives birth?"

I point at the tea, "Your followers call this the Golden Nectar. But no one actually knows what's in it."

"I know."

"Yeah, you know, but…"

"But you don't."

"I know what people pay for it. Your Golden Nectar got to be the most expensive drink in the history of the world!"

"It is my Magic Elixir. You know? But I only use it in High Sacraments, for my closest disciples."

"Yeah I know, I watch you, remember?"

Dreamer smiles with perverted joy.

I say, "I see people pay anything and sacrifice everything to do sacraments with you."

He says, "But not you."

"No, I'm special, aren't I?"

"You are indeed a unique character."

"Yeah, yeah, yeah, you need me don't you?"

The Dreamer gropes at himself like a shameless monkey. Exhibiting himself to me. Whining like a spoiled brat, "Look at me! Look at me!"

I say, "Yeah, you need me to watch you."

He is happy when my eyes are on him, "I have a good drink for you tonight. I made it myself."

I carefully turn over two cups, and pour for the Dreamer first. He motions for me to hook up to several lines of electrodes lying on the floor under the table.

I have to watch my attitude.

I hook up, and sip the special tea with the Dreamer.

He says, "There is an ancient Ayurvedic tradition in Hindu medicine, drinking your own urine for your health, like Gandhi did."

"Yeah, I think I saw that in a magazine at the Bodhi Tree Bookstore."

"Psychedelics are more effective after purification through a shaman's kidneys too."

I say, "Yeah, Indians did that with mescaline, but…"

Earthquake hits. Everything shakes and rolls.

The Dreamer braces for trouble, holding the tea secure.

I do nothing.

When the shaking stops, he loosens his grip on the tea, and asks me, "You know the new brain-scanners we've been using?"

"Yes Sir. I was told they give a precise picture of how human thoughts, emotions and behavior arise from the dynamic chemistry of the brain."

"Indeed! Precisely what I required."

I feel the intense pounding rhythmic notes and rapid drumming more and more.

He says, "I think it is working now."

"What?"

Dreamer is enjoying himself, being sly and evil.

"You want Allison? In the Buddha's Head?"

"What? But I thought… What did you say?"

"The Old Monk died. Your buddy Wai Yu is a catatonic pile of flesh."

Aftershock hits.

Dreamer braces again.

Then it's over.

"I don't care about the Old Monk, or Wai Yu either. I don't even care about Buddha's Head."

"Is that so? You don't care where Buddha's Head is?"

"No."

"You don't want to know what happened to it?"

"No. I don't care I said! I just want Allison."

"What if Allison is trapped inside the Head? Then do you care?"

"Wait, you took her? You saying you took Allison inside Buddha's Head?"

"I took the Head."

"I don't care about the Head anymore! I only care about Allison!"

"You only care about yourself! But there is no self, is there Mr. Genetic Free Man?"

I sit there.

"So how can there be anyone else? How can there be anyone else to love you?"

The Dreamer begins a creepy chant.

"There is no Allison.

It is all in the Head.

There is no Allison.

It is all in the Head."

Creepy and irritating.

"It is only in the head.

It is only in the head."

I say, "I just wanted Allison to love me."

He says, "Your destiny does not appear to include the satisfaction of your karmic desires."

"Why me? Why do you keep me here?"

"You thought you saw Allison and The Devil, but all you saw was me and you Genetic, just me and you."

"I can't, I can't just..." My mind is disconnecting, "What?"

I am losing it.

The Dreamer is phosphorescent, 3-D day-glow in black light.

"I'm flipping out. This is it, for real."

The Dreamer moves in on his prey with dilated eyes, coming close, inhaling my scent, whispering, blowing in my ear.

"Lift up my robes."

The Dreamer is licking my ear!

"Lift up my robes."

I fight the gag reflex, but now there is an exterior source of energy directing my nerves and muscles.

I watch helplessly as my body responds to the Dreamer's request.

I see Genetic awkwardly scoot around to the Dreamer's side.

"Yes, lift it."

The kimono fabric is an intricately woven, irresistibly beautiful landscape, filled with a mysterious radiance.

A pair of hands reaches for the hem and lifts slowly.

There is energy all around, pulsating and alive.

Something is there, underneath the robes. Visible, palpable energy. The rhythmic pulse of life. The source of everything.

The Dreamer rocks back and forth. Rotating and rocking.

"Go ahead. Lift it all the way up."

Genetic sees the forked tip of the Dreamer's pink meat tongue flap up and down, searching for a target.

The Dreamer isn't human anymore.

The hands lift the kimono higher.

The Dreamer has one of those masks of his own head with the Perfect Buddha's Head stuffed inside it, shoved up into his crotch, and he's twisting his torso around like a wound-up serpent.

The Dreamer's ugly penis is snaking up and wagging back and forth, like on a wild animal.

He says, "Yeah baby, I've got it all right here and now."

He is on the verge of frenzy. Twisting himself around and grinding on his own head.

"Figure out what you want Genetic. This is your last chance to get it, ever."

Reptilian scents fill the room, fear is everywhere.

The demonic Dreamer coils closer, lifts his robes all off.

***

The usually invisible snake is now visible, as it eats itself, loves itself, and regenerates again and again.

"You ask me, with a voice that sweats tears...

Do I know what love is?

Do I really know anything about it?"

Osiris is drowned in the dark depths of the Nile River, and dismembered.

His penis is cut into pieces and fed to three different species of sea creatures so it can never be found again.

Isis searches and searches for the pieces of her lover, until she can re-make his penis for him...

But she cannot give it life.

Isis mounts Osiris, bends her head to suckle at his breast. Flicks her tongue, pulls, pushes, and pinches until his nipples feel the phantom force of a mother's life-sustaining milk...

But still it is not enough.

The Lizard Lady asserts her True Self.

"I, and I alone, am enough."

I tell her, "I don't understand, I still don't understand. What can I do about death?"

She says, "Speak as I speak, Oh Aman-Ra, God of all Gods, let death be the doorway to new life."

I say, "But how can such things even happen?

How can *anything* happen?

Tell me, please, how can anything happen at all?"

"I, and I alone, am enough."

Then, I am awash in images of Ancient Gods, Stars, Pyramids, the Ultimate Scales of Justice, energy pouring down and shooting up, carrying human souls up and down.

She says, "All souls are cultivated for me.

All souls come to me."

The Lizard Lady smiles.

"Things happen for real, because I imagine them to happen for real."

"I, and I alone, am enough."

~25~

Freedom

Inside the Theater of the Absurd, there is a day-glow version of Washington DC on a dark stage.

The Sleeper is shot dead, as soon as he steps out of a crowd, on his way to the White House.

VCK patiently gets down on one knee, and takes new aim.

When the psychotronic snake rips through the air, VCK calmly fires another shot exploding through its head, secures his weapon, and starts walking away.

He says, "I had to do it. I'm the only one who could."

Everyone walks off the stage and all goes black.

There is nothing but one ill-defined lump left in the dark.

It is not the Sleeper. It is not the Snake.

It is Allison.

***

There is a sudden knock on the car door window.

VCK shows his credentials, "Back off."

The Police bow, back off.

VCK remains in the driver's seat, watching the Dreamer's window.

Just after 4:00 a.m. the glass bursts out. Someone jumps onto the roof, down to the ground, and runs away.

Vinney rushes over to where the jumper landed, climbs up on a wall and pulls himself onto the roof. It isn't easy anymore but he can still do it.

He crawls up to look inside the broken window.

Someone gives an injection to the screaming victim.

Medics load him onto a stretcher and hurry down the hall.

There, in the corner...

VCK goes for it, grabs the Perfect Buddha's Head.

Part Six: In The Here & Now

~26~

Is This Who I Am?

"I can't do it anymore. Everything is too fucked up. The whole world. It isn't my fault. The whole world is fucked the fuck up!"

The Lizard Lady tells me, "Death won't help you Genetic. You've made too many enemies already."

My soul is whooshed away into a ghost world filled with entities familiar and strange. But I cannot tell if I am dead or not. I really don't know anymore.

I see Gods, demigods, devils, demons, gurus, swamis and saints. Nostradamus, Swedenborg, Ramakrishna, Rajneesh, Bhaktivedanta, the goddess Ishtar, and the

151

great Shawnee Prophet. All the other characters, Madame Blavatsky, the Beast 666, Anton LaVey, Mary Baker Eddy, Joseph Smith, Cagliostro, Meher Baba, Sai Baba, and the Maharishi.

Dead or alive, it didn't matter.

Everyone is here.

Angel guides and impish little pranksters point down irresistibly curious but obvious dead ends.

Earth-toned vegetarian Mushroom People. Gaseous wisps of consciousness. Furies. Goblins. Tibetan tulpas, elves, gnomes, fairies, and satyrs. Larvae created in masturbatory fantasy by imaginary sperm. Tcheou-Wang, the Chinese God of Sodomy and patron of boy prostitutes. Gandharvas, a blood-sucking Hindu incubi.

"It never ends, does it?"

She says, "Our need to feed on ourselves is just as strong as our need to regenerate."

I see the Savior, millions of savior-wannabes, and millions more wanting to be saved.

I see parasites, germs and other odious malignancies of the spirit stretching the entire length of time, past, present and future.

I say, "We are The Serpent eating our own tail. I see it. I see all of us, all of humanity, we are The Serpent eating its own tail."

The Lizard Lady tells me, "Here and now, words are your only hope. The creative power of the primordial sounds as they coalesce into the phenomenal world."

Monks are chanting *A-U-M*.

"I search for my own truth. I find: The Mirror. I know who I am. I know what I must do."

She asks, "You do?"

"But I see so many people die again and again. I see people, I see life decay into inanimate matter!"

"Yes my dear and gentle one. The reality of your own immortality is completely up to you. You take it, or you leave it."

The Lizard Lady is surreal and serene.

I quiver at the sight of her overflowing warm flesh.

She is more real than reality.

Her power is inconceivable.

She tells me, "You can look into your true lover's eyes and see anything you want."

I look into her eyes.

She says, "I am what you always wanted to see."

I am awed.

She explains, "Power flows to the target of adoration from the souls of believers and devotees."

I got it! I got it!

"The Holy Conman. He runs this carnival!"

She says, "No mortal being has ever seen his face without dying."

"So how can I?"

She tells me, "You must know what you cannot know."

Then she smiles like when I first stuffed my hand under her bra, and says, "You know that by now, don't you?"

~27~

Is That Still Who I Am?

I am comfortably confined in a secure room in the basement of the U.S. Embassy in Tokyo.

They give me coffee, eggs over medium, with crisp bacon and extra well-done fries.

I have marine guards and a crack team of psychiatric and intelligence personnel to observe and evaluate everything I do or say.

The Psychiatrist asks me, "Is there anything else I can do for you?"

"Get me 30 x 32 jeans, 16 x 33 blue plaid flannel shirt, warm socks and boxers. I wanna dress like Neil Young for a change."

They record my entire story. All about Psytron, immortality. Regulator One, Elizabeth. The sleeper and the slug in his butt. Allison. Her suicide. Wai Yu in LA. My own escape to Bangkok. The Buddha's Head. The Holy Conman invading my body. Allison's abduction in the afterlife. The Lizard Lady, and her big white bra.

Twisted gods, demons, years of confinement and mind-control. Slugs with psychotronic power crawling onto my face, into and out of my body. Drugs. Sex. Secret plots. Golden Nectar. The Dreamer grinding around on the Perfect Buddha's Head with his ugly old penis flapping back and forth like a snake. The Lizard Lady watching over me.

"And my head was spinning from the Dreamer hypnotizing me."

"Yes…?"

"The Lizard Lady became me, or I became the Lizard Lady. I don't know how to explain it."

"Yes…?" The Psychiatrist listens carefully, taking notes too.

"Until that moment, physical violence against the Dreamer had simply been inconceivable."

"But now you decide to attack?"

"I don't know who decided what, but my hands are ready to grab his neck and open it up."

I use my hands to show how I'd do it.

"The Lizard Lady strikes first. She catches the snake in her teeth and bites down hard, whipping her head from side to side."

I show how she did it, whipping my head and hands all around.

He says, "The Lizard Lady?"

"The Dreamer claws at her face and eyes. But she is like the Goddess Kali. She has more arms and hands and mouths than any one man can control."

"So you say, Lizard Lady is biting his penis?"

"I grab the fucking tea and smash it into the Dreamer's skull."

I swing my arm fast and hard to show him. Bam!

"And you escape?"

"Oh yeah man, right out the fuckin' window…

Like my ass is on fire."

"I see."

I smile, "You don't see anything. But it's okay. I'm not crazy anymore. I mean, I know you can't believe me. It just doesn't matter what you think."

∗∗∗

A couple days later, there is loud thunder and lightning outside the White House.

Rain hits the windows.

Aides and other members of the emergency response team nervously wait around, unsure what to do as an uncharacteristically exasperated POTUS stares at me on screen.

I contentedly sip my French Roast Cappuccino and nibble on my crunchy chocolate-dipped Almond Biscotti.

POTUS finally gives up, "Okay. I'll call you 'The Acid Head Buddha' from now on."

"Thank you."

"Now are you happy?"

"Thank you Mr. President."

I reluctantly leave my Cappuccino and Biscotti on the table, and I tell the President of the United States, "We shall proceed."

I ask him again, "You are God in the First Act of Creation. What do you do?"

He says, "I give up, I'm God, what do I do?"

I say, "You explode in unlimited self-love.

The President says, "I'm God. I jerk off. I got it. Didn't I tell you that already?"

I continue to enlighten the President of the United States to the Ultimate Truth I have discovered.

"The Unformed Nothing imagines ONE GOD, the Great Androgynous Shemale, whose nature is to create *more*."

"One God imagines TWO and invents sex, masturbating to the orgasmic reality of two more Gods, male and female."

I feel rather proud of my own discourse and the good deed I am doing for my country and the whole world too.

"Wallah! There are THREE! Like the Holy Trinity. And the entire physical universe was necessary to make it happen."

He says more loudly, "I said I got it already! God jerks off, and numbers are invented too. Okay?"

I say, "All the seeds of nature and laws of physics are essential to create a reality in which two complimentary opposites attract each other and consume each other."

I wait a minute for The Truth to sink in to my listener's mind. Deciphering when he is ready to learn more. And then I continue.

"A reality in which energy equals matter, waves equal particles, light equals time, and nothing is ever as simple as it seems."

POTUS asks his aides, "What the fuck am I listening to? And why the fuck do I need to talk to this asshole?"

"*El correcto*," I say, "You don't need to hear any more than what you have just been told."

He says, "Finally!"

Thunderclap.

I say, "The Tower of Babel is not about people who can't understand each other because they speak different languages."

Aside again, "The fucker's still talkin' at me?"

I tell him, "We cannot understand each other even when we speak the same language."

The President says, "He is still fucking talking!"

$***$

The Lizard Lady tells me, "The cross is the oldest symbol in African religion."

A beautiful Nubian Goddess with powerful thighs and breast, dances in front of me and says, "You White people go to church and talk about God, but we Black people dance and become God!"

I tell the Nubian Goddess, "The cross is where the natural meets the supernatural."

She stops dancing. Looks in my eyes and says, "Sex is not just DNA's way of making more DNA."

I adore her already.

The Lizard Lady says, "The reality of sex is more dependent on the imagination than we imagine it to really be."

The Nubian Goddess says, "Imagination *is* reality."

I say, "Tell me, please tell me everything!"

The Lizard Lady says, "The Earth's insanity comes from the West. It is an Occidental form of malevolence that will destroy the world in time."

I listen.

"But it is a blameless thing.

It is no one's fault.

No White man. No Yellow man.

No Black man or Brown man.

No woman's fault.

No Government. Military. Capitalist.

It doesn't matter.

Blaming each other is just part of the problem."

I ask, "What about death? Immortality?"

The Nubian Goddess tells me, "You are the one whom the gods have chosen to give them better orgasms."

The Lizard Lady tells me, "There is nothing the gods won't do for you."

The Nubian Goddess whirls around. I see her vertebrae radiant in a line of visible energy snaking up her back to the base of her skull. But this is no ordinary skull. There is, balanced on top of her spine, another face.

It does not surprise me. Somehow it belongs there.

She looks at me looking at her.

She whirls again, and I see a long flaccid penis hanging over two hefty testicles.

This too, I cannot question. I am simply struck silent by her beauty.

She has arms and hands growing out in pairs now, two, four, six.

More breasts are growing before my eyes, two, four, six. Curvilinear spheroids tipped with meaty, burgundy, blood-filled protrusions, like little penises, all pointing at me.

She says, "Come, explore the unknowable pleasures I can give you."

Her thick tongue sticks out longer and longer. She could choke me with it. She could impale a man if she wants to. I tell her, "I'm ready to die, be devoured, become part of you."

She says, "I dare you. Become me. Not like me, not part of me. You become me!"

The tip of her penis is pointing back, climbing up the space between her bottom cheeks. There is a piquant pubic patch around a receptive sexual organ of a kind we can't even comprehend.

Mouth, anus, vagina, or what is it?

"Take my Existence."

She is penetrating, or merging into herself.

"Take my Karma."

Disappearing inside her own self.

"There is still more here, still more you haven't seen yet. Do whatever you will, but take it all before it is too late."

***

Back at the White House…

POTUS is in intense consultation with his team.

I appear on screen again, "Excuse me gentlemen."

They all look.

"My gypsy, my acid queen is here now to take me for my ride."

They can hear her too, "Come! Take it all."

I smile.

"I respectfully ask you, Mr. President, *El Capitano*, Spy Man, and Doctor of Psychiatry.

Where is your gypsy?

Where is your acid queen?"

I give the peace sign, say "Later."

***

A couple days after that, I'm in the Tokyo Imperial Hotel watching news, flanked by my newly acquired Lawyer, Accountant and Publicist Lady.

I sip the chocolate-powdered foam out of my second cup of French Roast Cappuccino even more irritatingly noisy than usual.

A Police Spokesman on TV says, "Actionable intelligence was gathered from an American individual who escaped after years of captivity and psychotronic mind-control."

The first in a gaggle of Reporters shouts out, "Were the girls raped?"

Police say, "We mobilized a massive force to catch the Dreamer unprepared."

Another one, "What about chemical weapons? His nuclear arsenal?"

Another Reporter shouts, "Who was the American?"

And another one yells, "What does psychotronic actually mean?"

Police say, "We believe we have confiscated the bulk of his chemical arsenal."

The first Reporter screams, "What about his penis?"

I tell my people, "Yo, dudes, watch this, watch this!"

Another Reporter says, "Would you say the chewing and ripping action on his penis was much nastier than a clean cut with a sharp knife?"

The TV shows the Dreamer being taken into custody with his penis pieces wrapped in white gauze, secured to his crotch like a Frankenstein cocktail wienie.

And I'm there on TV, yelling at him, "Look at me Dreamer! Look at me!"

The Dreamer obediently stares back into my new night vision camera with his hands going absolutely crazy trying to find his penis to hold onto.

My Publicist Lady says, "Brilliant, absolutely brilliant piece of film."

My Accountant nods agreement, "Clearly worth a fortune to any news organization in Japan."

My Lawyer says, "The way he looks at you..."

One of the Dreamer's Lawyers on TV says, "We are confident our client will be judged mentally incompetent to stand trial for the alleged crimes."

I tell the Reporter, "I concur with Counsel for the Defense. The Dreamer will spend the rest of his life in psychiatric facilities for the criminally insane... waiting for his penis to heal."

I smile, and give the peace sign on TV.

~28~

POTUS in the White House

It is somber and official in the White House today. Looks like the intelligence people have to explain a lot of bad news to POTUS.

The Agent Man says, "Mr. President, a drug-induced, virtual reality experience has been developed in Japan."

Agent Lady says, "They focus a psychotropic agent into the users brain with computer-directed chemical and electrical manipulation of the nervous system."

POTUS says, "I wonder how that might work."

The Man says, "No one seems to know exactly how that works yet, Sir."

Agent Lady clears her throat, "What happens next is apparently difficult to explain, Sir."

POTUS says, "Do you feel the bliss of mystic ego dissolution? Do you have an orgasm? Just tell me what happens."

Agent Man says, "The user comes back, neurologically redesigned. Some kind of a freak, I guess, with an electromagnetic field, and psychic power or something."

POTUS tells the Agents, "I'm starting to feel a little freaky here myself people..."

Agent Lady tells POTUS, "VCK says he saw one of the users with his own eyes and he had a visible field around him."

POTUS asks, "So, you want me to let you kill a man, because he has a halo? Or did you call it an aura?"

The Lady says, "Mr. President, due to the speed of reported developments and the clear danger to national security..."

***

A little while later…

POTUS is with the intelligence Agents and various Experts on various screens, including VCK from the US Embassy in Tokyo.

VCK says, "That's right. He had a visible electromagnetic field."

POTUS says, "You mean, you can see an electromagnetic field, but can other people see it too?"

The CIA Medical Expert on his screen says, "This is beyond hallucination or intoxication. It is like invasive surgery. A bio-chemical-electrical operation, on the user's brain."

Agent Lady says, "Someone has directed a staff of rogue Neuroanatomists, Psychogeneticists, and Molecular Biologists to use a fluorescent screening technique…"

POTUS asks, "A what?"

The CIA expert says, "A screening technique used in Targeted Genomics."

POTUS, "You think they found a genetic key that lets them get inside the brain?"

Agent Lady explains, "The Japanese say the DNA code is unlocked by a guidance system that customizes the drug's molecular structure as it is being absorbed into the circulatory system."

The CIA Expert agrees, "That analysis is not inconceivable."

VCK takes it beyond everyone's expectations, "You travel through time and space."

No one knows exactly what to say about VCK.

"You meet other beings, in other dimensions. Go to parallel worlds, alternate universes…"

POTUS must be the one to speak, "Um, you know, I don't care what people believe, but…"

The CIA Director aligns with POTUS. "What do these freaks actually do? Not what they think or imagine they do, but what do they actually do?"

VCK says, "That's the whole point boy! What they do, in fact, is imagine reality, for real!"

Whether he is crazy or not, no one wants VCK for an enemy.

POTUS simply must be the one to ask, "Vinney, what exactly are you talking about?"

Vinney walks out, smiling like no one ever saw before.

But no one else is smiling.

And no one dares to look in anyone's eyes.

~29~

The Invitation

A Zen Monk sits on a dirty sidewalk, dressed in black, thumping on a drum.

Japanese and *gaijin* on opposite corners take pictures of the same crowd crossing the same intersection.

Everything is familiar in Shibuya, except maybe me.

I step out of the station. Refreshed. Thinking, I'm super cool and fashionable again.

I wiggle my way around and through to the front of the crowd.

I like to walk fast, and I'm kind of excited too.

My friends try to follow as quickly as they can.

I look at the invitation in my hand. From Sayako, to me, personally! Delivered by the Three Virgins.

My lovely friends have grown up. They are beautiful, and dressed pretty for a fun night out.

We are going to see Sayako and God's Pussy perform her new CD, *Blind People Selling Porno*, at Shibuya Concert Hall.

✶✶✶

VCK sneaks up behind his target walking by a parked car in the super-congested intersection outside Shibuya Station.

One look in the eyes, and one touch is all he needs.

He throws me into the passenger seat, walks around to the other side, and gets in the car.

The Virgins cheer and wave goodbye, "*Ganbatte*, Generic Sensei! Fight on! *Ganbatte*!"

I try to talk.

He slaps a piece of tape over my mouth.

He starts driving away.

I try to talk, but can't.

✶✶✶

Sayako dances onto the stage in psychedelic shock-rock lingerie, and wearing traditional *geta* sandals, with cotton *tabi* two-toe socks.

She has solid gold sea serpents wound around her calves.

The audience is filled with young adoring fans of both sexes.

Stage lighting is precise as a medical procedure. Nothing happens by chance.

The stage is filled with indiscriminate piles of live people and inanimate mannequins.

Old Fat Guys in skin-tone spandex climb all over each other to pay obeisance to Sayako's rear-end.

They are just like the butt-sniffers in the bank robbery. They simply cannot get enough of the young lady's beautiful ass.

Hairless, oiled Body Builders with their groins wrapped in white *fundoshi*, like sumo wrestlers, ignore Sayako and everything else, to ogle and grope each other.

Sayako navigates the mass of bodies, dancing however she feels.

She fools, she frolics, and she maneuvers her way to the VIP section in the front row.

She sees the Three Virgins all right, but the man she wanted them to bring for her is not there in the empty seat.

Where is Genetic?

She makes a face at the Virgins.

~30~

The New Holy Trinity

I watch him driving.

He looks back at me once in a while.

Then, VCK finally says, "The tape, ya know...

I don't like to be mean but...

Come on boy, you just talk too much."

Okay, okay, I nod affirmative.

He says, "That's the spirit."

VCK reaches behind his seat, pulls out my good old purple bag, and hangs it on my shoulder.

I can feel my own eyes sparkle.

He tells me, "It isn't your fault. I know you love my daughter."

I feel like everything stops.

I'm watching him.

"Genetic Freeman, Vinney Cold Killer, and The Perfect Buddha's Head."

My eyes are wide.

"Yes, now, *we* are the Holy Trinity."

I shake my head vigorously, negative, negative.

"Oh, yeah, that's right..."

He is a sly fucker.

"I almost forgot..."

He starts laughing hilariously.

"You made the President of the United States call you the Acid Head Buddha!"

Yeah, I guess he liked that. I mean it was pretty funny, ya know, the President and all.

When Vinney calms down, he says, "We are the *New* Holy Trinity!"

Our eyes meet.

"The Perfect Buddha's Head, Vinney Cold Killer, and the Acid Head Buddha."

Yeah.

Now we are both satisfied.

We are both ready.

And we both try not to show we are more afraid than we have ever been before.

~31~

The Unstoppable Explosion

In the endlessness of Virgin Space, a single dot of light becomes a line…

And then a triangle.

The triangle is made of three spirits, a Trinity, with distinguishable colors and energy for each.

There is an unstoppable explosion of all possible geometry.

The THREE multiplies into millions of fractal images of self, multiplying into more millions, and billions, a raging White-Hot Star brighter than any in all the black sky.

Light is perfectly reflected onto each individual operator. Billions and billions of Beings in One, The Holy Conman.

The White-Hot Star dissolves into a blistering Black Hole that gives birth to a Singularity of undifferentiated fiery liquid, which congeals for one final instant.

Then, it is too late.

It is the perfect Cosmic Mirror.

The Holy Conman feels the illusion of his elaborate, infinitely complex hierarchy of beings start to shatter.

The Holy Conman sees a reflection of his own self, for the first time ever, exactly as it is, a fallacy of individuality vanishing as if it never existed.

A magnificent multi-dimensional pyramid of nothingness comes crashing down into itself, into oblivion.

~32~

The Theater of the Absurd

Everything is perfectly quiet.

The black carpet floor slopes down to a shadowy stage. The matte black ceiling has hints of phosphorescence from red-light exit signs: "Positively 4th Street," "Desolation Row," and "Back to Highway 61."

A thick curtain rises slowly, soundlessly above the empty stage. Uniform blackness differentiates into shades of dark gray.

One ill-defined lump remains lifeless and undisturbed.

A voice says, "Now, at this instant, I am here, in utter darkness."

The Sun begins to rise from stage right. Not stage lighting, but the Sun itself breaches the distant horizon and hits the Arch in Washington Square, sizzling all the way down.

"The Sun, the same Sun I have seen so many times before, but this Sun is even more majestic, more beautiful."

Birds begin chirping. Leaves are rustling in a breeze.

I say, "Listen."

Buh dum. Buh dum. Buh dum.

"Yes, the rhythm."

Buh dum. Buh dum. Buh dum.

The rhythm of life on Earth.

Buh dum. Buh dum. Buh dum.

The Sun grows bigger, brighter, until it cannot be endured.

"Genetic, is that really you?"

Allison feels a rain of playful electric tingles pulsing through her being. But there is so much more significance to it. So many questions are answered. So much fatigue is lifted. So much energy is set free.

I hear her say, "I needed to be somewhere only you could find me."

Beautifully complex rhythms of infinitely varied pulses, each one identifiable only for an instant, then and always, part of an ocean of light, no, bigger, a milky way, an unlimited cosmic flow, a...

＊＊＊

The Wicked Old Witch says, "Begin at the end."

I say, "There I am. I myself am pulsing for one infinite instant."

Slick Willie says, "Now begin at the end."

One Eye Johnny, crazy and laughing, says,

"The end is the beginning.

The beginning is the end.

Everything was over before it began."

＊＊＊

The fact is, it begins where it often ends, in a cold hard hospital room.

＊＊＊

"Sayako, beautiful, beautiful Sayako, push, push harder."

The baby's slick silver shoulders pop right out.

In another quick motion, his long arched back slurps all the way out.

I lean forward, and hold my breath.

Blood rushes to fill the spaces behind the baby's silver skin, his hips and legs are pulled along by his own momentum.

I am pushed back by a force I cannot see.

Breath is sucked out of my lungs before I realize it. I hear my own voice as it echoes in the antiseptic air.

"What comes after death? What is waiting for us in The End? And in The Final End?"

I cut the baby's umbilical cord, as it is presented to me, with the scissors a nurse has placed in my hand.

The medical team quickly checks and cleans my son on top of a stainless steel cart built and equipped for that purpose.

A nurse wraps the newborn baby inside a white cotton-soft blanket and hands him to the father.

I hear the Lizard Lady say, "You can look into your true lover's eyes and see anything you want."

The baby's eyes are squeezed shut, just as they'd been throughout his time in his mother's amniotic sac, but the lashes are already long and beautiful.

The left eye remains still as the right flutters open.

Then, soon enough, the left eye too flutters itself open.

I hand the baby to my gorgeous and wonderful wife.

"Here, look at his eyes."

The new baby's eyes sparkle with magical power.

Sayako is a blissful new mom.

I am a blissful new dad.

Then...

***

The martini glass falls first, and shatters on the floor.

Joan hits the floor next, still smiling, even with a bullet hole in the middle of her head.

The apple rolls to the fore.

The End

About the Author

Anthony Lojac was born and raised in and around NYC.

He rode his motorcycle cross-country, studied Philosophy and Law in LA, and then went to Tokyo to learn Japanese.

Ten years later, Anthony quit his job, bought a boat, and has been writing on the water as much as possible ever since.

Currently, he is usually working on his vintage 1969 Grand Bank's all-wood trawler in Marina del Rey.

Anthony writes fiction and nonfiction in English and Japanese.

Acid Head Buddha is his third novel.

www.lojac.net

Acid Head Buddha

Also available in Japanese

Written & Translated by Anthony Lojac

Published by: Think More Books, *Beverly Hills*

Copyright © 2015 by Anthony Lojac. All rights reserved.

Acid Head Buddha™ Anthony Lojac

www.thinkmorebooks.com

www.lojac.net